Dy. Lusion

Presents....

PAN

Chapter 1: Only the Beginning

Pan's breath coiled into the silver air, dissolving like a ghost's sigh as dawn bled reluctantly over Neverland. The forest shimmered with an otherworldly pulse, dew-slick leaves catching the light and reflecting it in eerie, shifting emeralds, as if the trees themselves remembered the taste of fire.

The ground quivered beneath him with subtle, unseen life; soft, beckoning voices slithered through the mist—half-song, half-lure, threaded with old secrets. Every sound carried the weight of a spell, a whisper of the island's ancient consciousness.

This was sacred land. Not merely alive, but awake. The Mermaids of the Lagoon, their silver tails flashing like liquid moonlight; the shrieking phantoms called White Shriekers, ghostly claws scraping against the dark; the sly, whispering fae with eyes like embers—all were woven into the same living tapestry.

Magic ran through their veins like blood through a beating heart, feeding the pulse of Neverland itself. Without them, the island would wither. Pan could feel it already, faint and trembling beneath the roots and rocks—a sickness curling around the island's spine.

Hidden deep beyond a mountain draped in perpetual shadow lay the Hangman's Tree—the black heart of the Lost Boys' dominion, veiled in thorns, shrouded in secrets older than memory. Pan never took the same path twice when returning home. The boys thought him paranoid, a ghost chasing shadows. But Pan knew better. Hook's eyes were always there, lurking somewhere beyond the leaves, burning with patient hunger.

Hook did not crave Pan's death alone. He desired dominion. The veins of the island, its creatures, its immortal heart—he wanted to drain it dry until all that remained was dust and silence.

The Lost Boys knew none of this. They still laughed and fought and dreamed beneath the stars, oblivious, believing Hook a madman consumed by vengeance. But Pan had seen the truth: boys stolen from the outskirts, scavengers who never returned, fae who vanished mid-flight. He had stopped sending anyone beyond the borders.

Now, he walked beside the faeries. Guarded them. Listened to their whispers, a language older than any word he had ever known. One, in particular, had become his compass in the encroaching dark—Bell.

Her light was sharp as cut glass, her laughter dangerous as wind over cliffs, her wings humming a music that haunted him. Together they traversed the dying wilds, her glow flickering like a heartbeat beside him, her voice speaking in a bright, chiming dialect only few could understand.

The others called her Tinker Bell—a name she despised, a cage of syllables imposed by gods long since gone. But to Pan, she was just Bell: wild, untamed, furious as a falling star. She believed no deity would save them. Only those who bled for Neverland could.

When the lagoon died, so did the mermaids' songs. Its glassy waters cracked to salt flats, voices swallowed by dust and grief. The Indian Camp, stripped of celestial guidance, could no longer mark time; scavengers crept closer with each passing year. The balance was fraying, thin as a spider's silk in the storm.

Then came Hook's new throne—a vast, glimmering airship of steel and shadow, hovering like an open wound in the sky. His ship no longer sailed the seas; it devoured the heavens, blotting out clouds and stars alike.

Two weeks after the lagoon fell silent, Pan walked its corpse alone. The forest moaned around him—trees weeping amber sap like slow tears, animals frozen as if carved from stone.

Even the fae's light dimmed, shadows thickening in reluctant corners. He followed the dying pulse of green to a cavern near the shore, the last glimmer clinging to its rim. He crouched there, silent, unseen.

Below, Hook's men labored beside things that had once been beautiful: twisted merfolk with gaping mouths, fae whose wings were shredded and useless, beasts reeking of oil and ash—all chained to labor, digging black ore from the island's heart. The stone glimmered with a dark, almost sentient light. Each strike of the pickaxe sent shivers through the ground, through roots, through Pan's bones.

It was no longer war. It was desecration.

Pan's pulse quickened. "He's not trading it," he murmured, voice low and cold, tasting the bitterness of inevitability. "He's hoarding it. But why?"

Bell hovered near him, her wings chiming like frost against glass. She answered in her native tongue, words sharp as icicles. "The ore isn't just metal, it's ... .something else." Pan understood. The ore wasn't mere metal—it was Neverland's blood. Its essence. Its soul.

Hook was stealing the magic itself.

And as they stood at the edge of the dying world, Bell's glow flaring with rage, Pan looked at her—the trembling light against the gathering dark—and for a heartbeat, he glimpsed what the island could still be.

But only if they fought.

Because if they failed, the last thing Neverland would remember was not a battle cry, but the quiet, shattering sound of its own heart breaking.

Chapter 2: The Way to The Birch Wood Tree

Pan exhaled softly, his breath a ghost curling into the chill of dawn, dissolving before it could stain the air. Below him, the cavern pulsed with that infernal light—black and red, throbbing like a heart trapped beneath stone.

The glow painted jagged shadows across the walls, shadows that seemed to twitch and breathe on their own. Nothing moved. No eyes followed him. Yet the hairs on his neck stood, stiff as wire; the feeling of being watched clung to him like a second skin. He stepped back from the ridge, silent as the creeping mist that swirled at his ankles.

Bell lingered where he had been, hovering, wings vibrating with a restless tension. Her gaze was locked on the cavern's rhythmic glow. The ore called to her, pressing against her chest with the weight of some half-forgotten memory, intimate and wrong.

It hummed in a language older than thought, whispering songs of deep pasts that stirred both wonder and dread. When she reached toward it, her fingers grazed nothing but air; the thought slipped through her hands like smoke, leaving a cold, hollow ache.

"Miss Bell?" Pan's voice broke the spell, warm and teasing against the oppressive dark.

He stood ahead, a boyish grin in sharp contrast to the gloom, smoldering mischief in his eyes. "You coming, or shall I leave you to court the shadows alone?"

Bell rolled her eyes, wings quivering with irritation—and something else. That grin of his always stirred a storm inside her, equal parts warmth and fury. "You're insufferable," she muttered, yet her glow flared once in the dark as she chased after him.

They moved through the forest in practiced silence, each step measured, careful. The air hummed with distant cries—the echo of creatures that had once sung and now only screamed. Beneath that, a subtle, fragile thread of intimacy lingered between them. They had danced this rhythm before: Pan, reckless and alive, forever one step from ruin; Bell, drawn to the edge, unable to turn away.

She had once followed him onto Hook's ship, slipping unseen through shadows and iron rigging. The scent of brine and oil clung to her like sin, sharp and unrelenting. To bear the stench of men, she kept Vidas close—fragile, blood-red blossoms plucked from the cliffs between Mermaid Lagoon and the Hangman's Tree. They smelled of endings: sharp, sorrowful, divine.

Hook had noticed once. She had dropped a single blossom onto his deck. He had picked it up with gloved fingers, turned it over, studied it, then tucked it into the black lace of his hat. No words. Just that thin, haunted smile. The memory unsettled her still. Hook's quiet was far more dangerous than his fury.

By the time she caught up, Pan crouched by a stream, gathering what the forest still offered: bowa fruit, garoni roots, the last surviving cepa bulbs. The forest's bounty was thinning fast. Fires were forbidden—light drew death from the skies—and the Lost Boys were learning to survive in shadows, feeding only on what the earth grudgingly yielded.

"The river's lower," Pan murmured, eyes tracing the sluggish water winding between grey stones. "If the rains don't return soon..." He did not finish. The thought tasted too much like defeat, bitter on his tongue.

As they walked the narrowing valley, Bell's silence grew heavier, a weight pressing against her chest. Her eyes drifted to the dying trees, the withered ferns, the ground littered with ash and brittle leaves. Her mind was elsewhere, lost to ghosts: Pixie Hollow.

Pan never asked about the fall of that place, but he knew the fragments—the tragedy that had torn the fae world apart. They called it The

Hollowing. Some blamed Lord Milori, some the gods. Those who whispered long enough all came to the same name: Beller Bell.

Restless, brilliant, starving for more than the Hollow could give, she had stolen Pixie Dust—sacred, intoxicating—until the Hollow bled dry. The Tree's heart had cracked the night she fled; the explosion of its dying magic burned the wings off every faerie who remained. Survivors became husks, wandering the woods in silence, empty-eyed. Pan had seen one once. Its wings were glass. Its mouth opened, but no sound emerged.

Bell never spoke of that night. But sometimes, when moonlight struck her just so, he could see faint lines along her back where light no longer shone through her wings. And now, even she was fading.

The Lagoon had died. The Mistri—sea-born beings of salt and starlight—were hunted for their glowing hearts. Hook's men lined the cavern walls with their corpses, turning the sacred into spectacle. The air reeked faintly of brine and rot.

Pan's jaw tightened. "He's killing the island," he said. "Piece by piece."

They walked until the moon rose, pale and cold. The silence between them deepened, not empty but weighted, like the pause before confession. Finally, Pan asked, "What did you see down there?"

Bell hesitated. Fingers danced through the air in careful, deliberate signs.

"The ore... it felt familiar. But I don't know why. It's old, Pan. Older than Neverland. Wrong." Her voice barely rose above a whisper. "Did you feel it?"

Pan shook his head. "No. I was watching the workers, not the stone. Tomorrow, I'll look again."

She nodded, unease, shading her features. The river whispered beside them as they crossed the shallows, water thin, cold, biting. Pan reached out, offering his hand. She paused, then took it, a fraction of a heartbeat.

Her palm was warm. His fingers curled around hers, rough with soil and salt. In that fleeting touch, something unspoken passed between them—a promise, perhaps, or a warning.

Above, the stars burned faint and distant. Mountains loomed like sleeping beasts, and the air itself seemed to hold its breath.

They were close to home—the Hangman's Tree waiting, a heart still beating in the dark.

But Bell glanced back toward the cavern and shivered, feeling the ore's pulse beneath her ribs, slow and patient, like something ancient waking from a long sleep. Deep down, though she did not yet understand why, she feared that when it woke, it would remember her.

Chapter 3: The White Shrieker

The forest's edge loomed like a threshold between life and nightmare. Mist coiled in tendrils around gnarled roots, stretching toward them as though craving warmth, whispering secrets in a tongue older than memory.

The dying light bled gold through the canopy, but even sunlight felt cold here, slanting across the twisted trunks in streaks of iron. Ahead lay miles of dark paths, thorn-choked glades, and beasts that should have been lost with the first age of Neverland.

Pan drew Bell up the last ridge, fingers tight around hers, pulling her from the bramble that tore at her skirts and hair. The only proof they still lived was the sharp sound of tearing leaves and her ragged breath.

He let her go only to draw his blade—iron dulled by years of battle, yet still hungry, still alive with the memory of blood. Silence pressed close, thick and suffocating, broken only by the low hum of Bell's magic.

Pixie Dust clung to her skin like a memory of firelight, soft gold bleeding through the gloom. That faint glow made her something both divine and dangerous, fragile and untouchable. Pan knew that beauty could kill them; light was always a lure, and in this place, predators were patient.

"If this were a fairytale," he muttered, voice low, edged with irony, "we'd travel in perfect darkness."

Bell glanced at him, eyes sharp, silent acknowledgment in the shadowed gold of her glow. Fairytales were dead things now, and both of them knew it.

The forest murmured around them—low, guttural howls threading through the trees, punctuated by shrieks that could not entirely be called human. Somewhere ahead, something was being torn apart. Pan's grip on his blade tightened as he stepped over a fallen trunk and extended his hand. She took it wordlessly, though her eyes were elsewhere, haunted, distant, listening to echoes only she could hear.

She had been fading for weeks. Her light flickered unevenly, her laughter vanished, her touch cooler than it once was. Whatever darkness was devouring Neverland had begun to consume her as well.

They pressed deeper, where trees twisted like broken bones and the ground soured beneath their boots. The air thickened with rot and decay. A swamp loomed ahead, rank water pooling in shadowless hollows. The smell of drowned leaves and stagnant life clung to their clothes and hair.

Then came the sound.

A rustle.

A beat of air.

Pan's instincts flared first—a vibration in the earth, a sudden chill crawling along his spine. His head snapped upward just as the creature broke through the canopy.

A White Shrieker.

Its wings unfurled like torn parchment; eyes burned with frozen fire, and its scream was the sound of glass shattering inside a skull.

"Run!" Pan hissed, gripping Bell's wrist.

The creature dove, a pallid specter in half-light. Bell blinked out of her trance, gasping as its claws shredded treetops. She darted behind him, wings trembling against the rush of wind that lashed their faces, scattering ash and leaves.

They crashed through undergrowth, branches clawing at skin and cloth, the Shrieker's cries tearing the air. The path forked—sheer ravine to the left, swamp writhing with unseen horrors to the right. Pan's eyes flicked to the left. "That way!"

Bell hesitated, fear anchoring her momentarily, but the creature's screech shattered doubt. They ran. The slope crumbled beneath them, sending them tumbling into moss and jagged stone.

Pan struck the ground hard, stars bursting behind his eyes, but rolled to his feet as the Shrieker swooped again. Its stinger flashed like a blade of ice. He swung—dull iron biting a shallow line into its tail. The beast shrieked, thrashing in fury.

"Keep running!" he roared. "Toward the bird rock! There's a cave under its beak—go!"

Bell's heart hammered as she sprinted, wings quivering with effort. The air reeked of rot and iron; behind her, the creature's shadow swallowed the trees whole.

Pan's shout echoed through the clearing, metal clashing, wings cracking against stone. She turned in time to see him stagger, blood blooming crimson down his arm.

"Pan!"

"Go!" he snarled.

Every step away felt like tearing a piece of herself free. The rock appeared—a centuries-carved eagle, its head bowed as if mourning. She ran toward it, voice breaking, "Here! Hurry!"

The Shrieker dove one final time. Pan twisted to strike, but the monster was faster; its claws raked his shoulder, and a cry froze her heart. Still, he ran—half-stumbling, half-dragging himself forward.

"DUCK!" Bell screamed.

Pan rolled, stinger sweeping inches from his neck. He dove into the cave just as the Shrieker collided with the eagle's beak. Stone splintered, wings shredded; the carved head crumbled in a rain of dust.

Bell caught him as he fell, arms wrapping around him with desperate strength. The cave trembled, the entrance collapsing behind them in a storm of dust, stone and shadows. Silence followed—a deep, suffocating silence broken only by ragged breaths and the faint, trembling shimmer of Pixie Dust.

Pan slumped against the wall, blood slicking his side. "I'm fine," he rasped. "Glad you're—"

Her hands struck his chest—not to hurt, but to stop him. Her eyes burned with unshed tears as she signed sharply: *You could've died. I almost lost you.*

Pan froze, chest heaving. Slowly, he lifted a hand, brushing her chin until their gazes met. Voice rough but steady: "Better me than you. Besides… it'll make a fine scar." He forced a grin, blood staining his fingers.

Bell let out a shaky laugh, half anger, half relief. "Idiot," she whispered, pressing her forehead to his. Her light dimmed, magic curling weakly around them like a dying flame.

Outside, wind howled through the ruins, carrying the distant cry of the Shrieker—wounded, but not dead.

Pan's eyes pierced the cave's black heart, where no light dared to linger. He could feel something moving beneath the stone, a slow, ancient heartbeat.

"Well," he murmured, raising his blade, "no going back now."

Bell's hand found his again—small, trembling, but certain.

And as darkness swallowed them whole, the only light left was the faint, golden shimmer of a dying star trapped between their palms.

Chapter 4: The Shadow Caves

Their footsteps whispered through the cavern, soft and steady as a lullaby sung to the bones of the earth. The air was cold and damp, clinging to skin like memory, heavy with the scent of wet stone and something older—something ancient and patient. Each breath Pan drew escaped as a ghostly wisp, curling in the dim, wavering glow.

Across the cavern walls, lights shimmered—blue and gold, like distant stars drowned beneath the sea—trailing after them as if the cave itself were breathing, watching. Bell's eyes caught their shimmer, wide and luminous, reflecting the hidden language of the stones, secrets spoken only to those willing to listen.

Behind them, the ocean murmured—an endless, unseen heart that throbbed beneath the world. Its deep rhythm was one of the few places Pan still felt peace, a pulse older than himself. The caves were alive with old magic: solemn, protective, resonating softly with echoes of those who had once called Neverland home, lingering in the air like a memory too persistent to forget.

Pan pressed his palm to the wound on his shoulder, the blood darkening the fabric of his tunic. He sank to one knee, breath shallow, rifling through his satchel with trembling fingers. Bell hovered near, her glow faint and tremulous, like candlelight flickering in a storm.

At last, Pan drew forth a single Aaslard flower, white as spilled moonlight, its golden pollen shimmering faintly. A healer's bloom, rare and sacred. He pressed it to the wound, hissing as the bloom's magic seeped into the cut, warm and biting, knitting flesh in a slow, deliberate rhythm.

The rope trembled in his hands as he tried to bind the wound, frustration etching his face. Bell floated closer, the air around her vibrating softly, faint chimes echoing with each movement of her wings. Without a word, she took the rope, fingers deft and precise, tying it tight. Her touch was soft, yet the strength beneath it surprised him.

Pan exhaled, half in pain, half in gratitude. He looked up at her, lips curling faintly in a silent sign: *Thank you.*

Bell's smile was small, shy, radiant—a flicker of warmth in the cavern's gloom. For a long moment, neither spoke. The only sound was the rhythmic drip of water echoing through the dark, like a heartbeat neither of them dared to name.

"You're the only person I know," Pan murmured, voice low, "who gets lost staring at cave lights."

Bell tilted her head, eyes bright with quiet mischief. "Maybe you've just never looked closely enough," she said.

He huffed a laugh, glancing upward. The cave ceiling shimmered with a thousand dying stars, veins of pale light tracing the rock like threads of liquid silver. "They're not just lights," he murmured. "They're Soultaurs. Spirits of the lost children. Dancing forever in the dark."

Bell's smile faltered, awe widening her eyes. "Children?"

He nodded, voice low, reverent. "They were like us once. But when the island took them—when the magic couldn't save them—they became this. Joy without pain. Light without memory."

A soft silence settled between them, heavy with reverence, echoing in the shadows.

"That's why I admire them," she whispered. "They never learned sorrow. They only ever learned how to glow."

Pan turned to her, truly seeing her—the curve of her cheek, the threads of gold in her hair, the fierce, quiet gentleness that set her apart. Words tangled in his throat; instead, he reached out, resting his hand on her shoulder.

"You always find light," he said. "Even when there's nothing but shadow left."

Her gaze lifted to meet his. For a heartbeat, time stilled. The Soultaurs' ghostly glow framed them, and he thought she looked less like a faerie and more like a fallen star, wild and burning to stay bright.

Then laughter shattered the spell.

The Soultaurs danced around them, spiraling in ribbons of gold and blue, their joy echoing through the hollow chamber like music made of glass and wind. Bell twirled among them, her laughter chiming, reckless and free, stirring the lights into frenzied ribbons. Pan watched, arms crossed, a reluctant smile tugging at his mouth.

When she finally stopped, breathless and beaming, she called to the lights above: "I'll come back soon! But I have to return my knight to his castle before he collapses!"

The spirits answered with a chorus of shimmering giggles. Pan rolled his eyes. "Knight?" he echoed, mock offense in his tone.

Bell grinned over her shoulder. "You do have the brooding part down."

He snorted, following as she led the way deeper into the cave, the path lined with veins of violet light pulsing faintly beneath the rock. The air grew warmer, scented with moss, salt, and a hint of magic older than time.

At last, sunlight spilled through the cave's mouth. Pan blinked against the brightness, stretching as he stepped into it. Beyond, trees swayed gently, whispering his name in the wind.

"It's good to be home," he murmured.

Bell darted ahead, spinning once in the sunlight. Her laughter rang like a promise, scattering across the clearing. Pan followed, and when she turned suddenly, he walked backward, smirking.

"You ready to go?" he teased.

"Hey—!" she yelped, chasing him.

He took off running, and her laughter followed—bright, wild, alive—spilling into the air like scattered starlight.

For the first time in a long while, the shadows in Pan's heart felt just a little lighter, and the world, if only for a moment, seemed to breathe with them.

Chapter 5: Back Home!

The forest's howl rose like a chorus of distant wolves, echoing through the mist that clung to the trees in ghostly ribbons. Pan ran, boots sinking softly into damp moss, Bell close behind, arms laden with vegetables that glimmered faintly in the moonlight, as if the earth itself had blessed them. The air smelled of wet leaves and faint smoke, heavy with the memory of fires long since burned.

Ahead, the Hangman's Tree loomed—a living monolith, massive and ancient, its bark twisted and pulsing faintly as though it bore its own heartbeat. As they neared the clearing, the boys' laughter rang out, wild and untamed, threading through the mist like sunlight breaking through storm clouds.

Pan's grin widened, fierce and unrestrained, as he stepped into the clearing. He threw his arms wide, laughter spilling from his chest, echoing across the grove. The Lost Boys swarmed around him like a whirlwind of motion—shouting, shoving, embracing, alive and unbroken. For a fleeting moment, the shadows seemed powerless to touch them.

"Welcome back, Peter!" a voice cried, high and eager.

Pan turned toward it, eyes bright as emerald fire, voice carrying a mock sternness. "Glad you're all alive and well. How's camp?"

"The camp is secure!" one of the taller boys barked, standing stiffly, shoulders square, a self-appointed sentinel. "Safe to play in!"

Pan chuckled, masking the weariness in his bones behind a boyish grin. Bell lingered at the edge of the clearing, watching him, her glow flickering softly, tentative and golden. There was something achingly tragic in the way he smiled—the way he carried the weight of their world and made it look effortless. His heart bled quietly for everyone but himself.

When he called out, "Who's ready for some Garoni?" the boys erupted, voices bouncing off the cavernous roots of the Hangman's Tree. Bell's lips curved softly, and she followed him to the long tables beneath the roots, the tree's hollow interior alive with shifting shadows and the scent of damp earth.

Pan moved with rough grace, slicing vegetables with his dagger and handing each boy a Garoni and a Bowa Fruit. The air thickened with the earthy scent of crushed herbs, rich and grounding. Bell hovered nearby, hands folded, declining his offer of food. She preferred to watch him—the subtle tension in his jaw, the way firelight caught the edges of his hair, the unspoken stories etched into his movements.

Once the boys had vanished into their chambers, Pan gathered what remained and returned to her. The night air had thickened, cool and heavy, smelling faintly of moss and mist. He reached into the supply bin, pulling out bandages and a wilted flower still tied to his shoulder.

"Would you mind?" he asked quietly, eyes glinting in the low light. "I'd do it myself, but I can't reach."

Bell said nothing, simply stepping closer until he could smell the faint sweetness of her magic—like crushed mint and starlight. As she untied the rope, the flower crumbled to ash, then trembled back to life, pale and delicate as a newborn breath.

Her fingers brushed his skin—light as breath, yet enough to make his pulse stumble. She soaked the new Aaslard flower in water and dabbed its juices onto his wound. The sting made him flinch, but the warmth that followed was nearly unbearable, a molten reassurance.

"Pan," she murmured, voice soft as falling ash, "you should have been more careful."

He laughed under his breath, quiet, almost rueful. "If it meant keeping you safe, I'd bleed again."

Her hand froze mid-motion. Eyes wide, lips parted as if to protest—but the words never came. He smiled, weary yet unflinching. "You know I would, Bell."

For a heartbeat, the air between them changed, fragile and electric. She wrapped the bandage around his shoulder, fingers trembling now. "You're impossible," she whispered.

He leaned slightly closer, voice dropping into a low growl. "So are you."

When she tied the last knot, he caught her wrist before she could pull away. Her wings quivered, scattering motes of gold into the dim light, ephemeral sparks against the shadows.

"Something's bothering you," he murmured. "Tell me."

Bell hesitated, gaze darting to the floor, then the flood came—anger sharp and raw, frustration braided with fear. Her hands moved in rapid signs, voice trembling with fury and something deeper: "I clean. I mend. I tell the boys your stories. But I am never allowed to fight beside you! Every time you go out, you get hurt—and I'm here, useless!"

Her words struck like lightning, but he did not flinch. He just looked at her quietly, the shadow of a smile softening his features. "You think you're useless?" His voice dropped, low and rough. "Bell, you hold this place together. You keep their spirits alive. You keep me alive."

He stepped closer, breath warm against her temple. "If you fell—if the island took you—I'd lose more than a friend. I'd lose the only light left in this cursed place."

Her heart fluttered painfully; she could not meet his eyes.

"I let you come with me today," he continued, fingers still wrapped around hers, "because I knew you were tired of being trapped. But you must understand, Bell—my recklessness is not bravery. It's the only way I know to keep the darkness away from you."

Silence followed, fragile as spun glass. She exhaled slowly, anger bleeding into reluctant acceptance. "Then at least make some of them help clean," she muttered, trying for levity.

Pan smiled, low and aching, a smile that did not quite reach his eyes. He brushed her hair aside, fingers lingering, warmth lingering too long. "I'll see what I can do, my little storm."

She froze at the words, wings fluttering softly. He chuckled, withdrawing his hand. "Thank you, Bell."

As she turned away to clean, Pan watched her go—light spilling from her wings, gold against the dark. Outside, the forest whispered again, leaves brushing his name from the treetops.

When night fell and the boys slept, Pan stood watch beneath the stars, one hand resting lightly on his bandaged shoulder. He could still feel the warmth of her touch, like the ghost of fire beneath his skin, and for the first time in days, the shadows in his heart felt just a little less heavy.

Chapter 6: The Gentle Moon

Pan stood at the edge of the watchtower, eyes fixed on the horizon where moonlight kissed the treetops, silver spilling across the island like liquid frost. The sea shimmered beyond, molten glass fractured by ghostly silhouettes of restless waves.

Wind tangled through his hair, cool and salt-sweet, carrying whispers of distant storms and salt-brined memories. He breathed it in, steadying himself on the precipice of something almost like yearning, the quiet ache of a world poised between wonder and decay.

With a soft exhale, he flicked his dagger into the air—silver catching silver—and let it fall, the motion flawless, practiced, beautiful, almost a dance. His hand rose just in time to catch the hilt before the blade could bite into the wood. The forest held its breath.

Below, the boys slept, the tents rising and falling with the rhythm of dreams. Pan leaned back against the rough bark of the old tree, eyes closing briefly, listening to the silence. Once, laughter had filled these woods—bright and reckless, like firelight dancing across the canopy. Now, the quiet pressed close, intimate and lonely.

The air shimmered. Tiny lights drifted through the branches—fireflies, or perhaps remnants of something older. Green, gold, violet—they hovered like dying embers from a god's forgotten hearth, their wings translucent as spider silk, movements deliberate, reverent. Not alive, not really. Memories pretending to be light.

Pan watched them, lost in the ache of remembering. The moons had been slipping away from the world for years, taking pieces of the island's magic with them. Even Neverland, eternal as it seemed, could fade.

Then, movement—fluid, silent. From the treeline, a tall, luminous figure emerged, runes cascading down its neck in a soft, living glow. The earth seemed to inhale and hold its breath.

The Night Stalker.

Once one among thousands—beasts of starlight wandering between worlds—now the last. Pan straightened, pulse caught between awe and grief, the weight of the island pressing against his chest.

A touch grazed his shoulder. Warm. Human.

He startled, hand snapping to his dagger. "I suggest you say something next time," he muttered, half-laughing, adrenaline sharpening his words. "Unless you want to get stabbed."

A faint, musical chime answered—a laugh like glass bells. Bell stood close, starlight spilling across her face, glinting in the gold threads of her wings.

"You know I can't just speak whenever I like," she signed, mock flourish in every gesture, grin soft but radiant.

Pan shook his head, tension melting from his shoulders as he leaned closer, close enough to smell her—wild, warm, like rain on stone. Bell rolled her eyes, but the corners of her mouth betrayed a smile.

Neither of them noticed the Night Stalker approach.

It moved like mist—massive, radiant, alive. When it halted before them, the air seemed to hold its breath. Bell's hands froze mid-sign as the creature's luminous muzzle brushed her stomach—so gentle it almost wasn't touched at all. Her breath hitched; Pan's pulse stumbled.

Pixie Dust bloomed across her skin, delicate and glittering like frost under moonlight. The runes on the Night Stalker's body flared brighter, and the world pulsed in tandem with her heartbeat. A soft wind rose, carrying scents of meadows and something deeper, sacred, older than memory.

Bell's eyes closed, utterly undone for a heartbeat, and Pan watched her—this fragile, impossible being bathed in lunar fire—something inside him cracking open.

When the Night Stalker turned and slipped silently back into the trees, the lingering wind was soft as silk. Bell's hair floated around her face, and Pan wanted, irrationally, to reach out and touch it.

For long, sacred moments, neither spoke. The silence was holy.

Then she turned, cheeks flushed, eyes bright with wonder. His throat tightened.

"Did you get a blessing?" he asked, voice tight, grinning to mask the weight in his chest.

She squealed soundlessly, hands flying in rapid, joyful bursts, starlight spilling from her every gesture. Her eyes glistened—bright, wet, alive.

Pan leaned against the tree, a ghost of a smile on his lips, yet his eyes carried the weight of all he'd seen, all he feared.

Later, after the forest stilled again, he dozed against the bark. Bell worked beside him, humming in tiny, melodic breaths, shaping a delicate figure from seeds and vine pods. Her movements were tender, almost motherly. When Pan stirred and saw her creation, she blushed, eyes darting up under his gaze.

"It's an autumn fairy," she signed, shy, voice lost in gesture. "If they were real."

Pan crouched beside her, knee brushing hers. The world narrowed to that point of contact.

"Beautiful," he whispered softly, and she wasn't certain whether he meant the fairy—or her.

Her smile faltered, then deepened.

He hesitated, then pulled her into a quiet embrace. She melted into it—brief, electric, the kind of closeness that lingered long after it ended.

"Why not," he murmured against her hair, "let's show it to the Soultaur caves."

When he pulled back, her eyes glistened; she cradled the tiny fairy as though it were sacred.

The first touch of dawn lit the sea. Pan tilted his head toward the horizon.

"Come on," he said. "We'll catch the sunrise before the others wake."

Bell followed, clutching her fragile creation. Together, shoulder to shoulder, they stood as the sun spilled gold over the island—two souls bound by wonder and something unspoken, watching the light finally find them.

Chapter 7: The Foggy Lake

Mist clung to the lake like a living thing, curling across the surface in delicate tendrils, heavy and cold as breath on glass. The boat drifted through it, slow and silent, its dark hull cutting through water that shimmered faintly beneath the moon, as if the stars themselves had fallen and were drowning. The boys' laughter floated around Pan in fragile bursts—bright, fleeting warmth against the vast hush of the lake.

He stood at the stern, muscles taut and movements deliberate, guiding the boat with the long ore like a gondolier ferrying souls across an underworld of shadows. Each push sent ripples across the black surface, silver ghosting in the moonlight. The fog thickened, blurring the edges of the world; trees and stars alike seemed suspended in a soft, timeless grey.

Beneath them, something ancient stirred. The Kobold slept here, deep in the lake's shadowed heart, dreaming the slow, endless dreams that shaped Neverland's tides. Pan had glimpsed its vast shadow once—a glimmering colossus that moved like liquid night. It was said to be harmless, unless roused—but in Neverland, nothing harmless came without a price.

He glanced down at the boys. They played pirates, brandishing sticks like swords, shouting and "dying" in exaggerated theatrics. Their joy was pure, untarnished by the truths Pan carried in his eyes. Children always believed they would never grow up, and he, of all creatures, knew the lie at the core of that hope.

A low groan rolled across the lake. The boys froze mid-play. Pan's grip tightened on the ore, every instinct on alert. The sound came again—deep, resonant, like the earth itself sighing in its sleep.

He knelt before Marmaduke and Fox, whispering gently. "I heard you two talking… about bringing someone back to camp?" His voice was steady, calm, but threaded with something older—history, warning, love.

Marmaduke fidgeted. "We just wanted Uzumati to play with us," he murmured. Fox looked away, guilt flickering like shadows in firelight.

Pan's sigh was soft, heavy with centuries. He rested a hand on Marmaduke's shoulder—firm, grounding, almost paternal. "You know he cannot leave his people. The roots of his spirit are tied to his home. Take him from that, and he'll lose the essence of who he is."

He drew them closer, voice dropping to a reverent hush. "You can make new bonds... but they'll never taste quite the same."

The boys nodded, chastened. Pan smiled faintly, brushing a thumb across Marmaduke's cheek before standing. "Now—go save Captain SBelly before he sinks the whole ship."

They scampered off, laughter returning like sunlight through clouds. Pan lingered, alone with the fog and the ache between what he said and what he felt. Too many souls had lost their homes, too many forgotten who they were meant to be.

He dipped the ore back into the black water and began to sing under his breath—an old chant learned from the lake's people. Low and resonant, it carried through the mist like a prayer, vibrating against the bones of the earth. The boys quieted, listening. Even the fog seemed to hold its breath.

Then—a ripple.

From the depths, a shadow rose, scales glimmering violet and blue, eyes vast and unblinking. The Kobold surfaced, magnificent and terrible, a god half-forgotten. Its head lowered, massive and graceful, single horn gleaming above the water. A sound rolled from its throat—soft, curious, almost hesitant.

Tootles stepped forward, trembling. "Careful," Pan murmured, hand brushing his shoulder instinctively. The boy froze.

The creature leaned closer, impossibly, pressing its snout against his palm. Pale blue light shimmered across their skin. For a heartbeat, the world stopped.

Pan's hand stayed on Tootles, but his gaze never left the Kobold—breath steaming, eyes ancient and knowing. He felt a pulse ripple through him, older than the island, older than himself. Then, as silently as it came, the Kobold sank beneath the water.

The boat lurched forward, carried swiftly by the lake's hidden currents. When they reached the far shore, the fog parted like silk. Firelight flickered between the trees, warm and gold, casting moving silhouettes—the people of the Indian camp dancing in welcome. Smoke, honeyed herbs, and earth mingled in the air.

Pan leapt from the boat, boots sinking into soft sand. He tied the rope, turned to help the boys climb out. Then—she appeared.

Tiger Lily.

Her shadow stretched long across the firelight, flames dancing in her dark eyes. Moonlight crowned her hair; braids threaded with silver and bone.

"Pan," she said, voice soft as smoke and dusk.

He bowed slightly, the ghost of a smile tugging at his mouth. "You haven't changed."

"Neither have you," she replied, stepping closer. The air between them was heavy, charged with memory and something unspoken, more dangerous than either dared acknowledge. Her fingers brushed his wrist—a spark against skin.

He almost took her hand. Almost.

But the boys watched, fire crackled, and Neverland itself seemed to pause.

"Come," she said, turning toward the campfire. "The feast waits."

Pan lingered a heartbeat longer, eyes tracing her retreating form, feeling the pulse of the island beneath his feet—the same rhythm thrumming in his chest whenever she was near.

When he finally followed, it was not just the promise of celebration that drew him. It was her. And the quiet, perilous truth that, for all his eternal youth, she made him feel mortal.

Chapter 8: Tiger Lily

The firelight flickered across Tiger Lily's bronze skin as she approached the boys, a soft glow dancing along her sharp, serene features. Her smile was gentle yet shadowed, hinting at the weight she carried even in ritual.

She sank to her knees with the grace of water flowing over stone, deliberate and reverent, a motion both commanding and tender. The boys mirrored her, heads bowed, hands trembling slightly as if the act itself demanded their devotion.

Tiger Lily's hands were warm as she took each boy's palms in hers, fingers curling around theirs with quiet assurance. She whispered prayers in a language that seemed older than the island, her voice soft and musical, leaving the words to linger like smoke in the heavy night air.

When she finished, she pressed a small symbol to each boy's forehead. Her thumb left faint traces of red—blood or pigment, it was impossible to tell—which glimmered in the firelight like tiny sparks of sacred fire.

Pan observed from a short distance, his gaze steady and intense. One arm crossed over his chest, the other slipping behind his back, posture elegant and controlled, every movement precise and instinctive. "Thank you for welcoming us to your camp," he said, voice low.

Tiger Lily straightened, eyes catching his in a collision of amber and emerald—sunlight and storm entwined. "Anything for the Prince of Neverland and his guests," she replied, her tone careful, soft, reverent, yet threaded with something personal that went beyond ritual.

The people of Le Clan de L'Aura Radieuse had long revered Pan—worshipped him, in quiet devotion, since the moment he had appeared from the mainland: a child of prophecy, destined to save Neverland with one act of pure selflessness. They had made him divine, though he never asked for adoration. Now, as she bowed to him, her reverence carried a pulse that felt human—yearning, perhaps even something tender and dangerous.

She stepped closer, so near that he could see the gold flecks shimmering in her irises, tiny suns trapped in her gaze. Her fingers brushed against his palms as she clasped his hands in both of hers. "I have nothing to offer but shelter and food," she murmured, lowering her head, the words delicate, almost vulnerable.

A familiar ache stirred in Pan's chest—a wordless ache he felt whenever she looked at him with such devotion. He tightened his grip, thumbs brushing her knuckles in a fleeting caress. "You know I never ask for offerings from your people," he whispered. "Only peace."

She lifted her gaze, and the lamplight caught the gold threads along her lashes, casting them like falling sparks. Pan released her hands too quickly, afraid she might sense the hesitation trembling behind his composure. "Come," he said, turning toward the boys. "Let's bring them to camp. These two cannot wait to find Uzumaki."

Tiger Lily nodded, guiding them through the village. Smoke from the cooking fires curled into the dusky sky, carrying the scent of roasted meat, herbs, and the ever-present salt of the sea.

Women moved gracefully between tents, sewing hides, tending flames, while children darted barefoot across the sand, laughter echoing like wind over water. Pan noted the absence of men—an uneasy, empty silence threaded through the vibrant life of the camp.

She pointed out the new fortifications along the perimeter: sharpened wooden spikes, stones laid with meticulous care, defenses that spoke of loss and vigilance. Pan's gaze darkened. "Where have the other men gone?"

Her hand froze midair, composure faltering for a heartbeat. A strand of hair brushed back, fingers lingering, before her voice came, low and steady:

"Hook's men have been taking our young, especially those who are coming of age." Her jaw tightened. "They leave us the old, the sick. The rest... they take."

Pan drew in a breath, heavy, but said nothing. Firelight carved her grief into something almost holy, etching it into the shadows around her.

They reached her tent—the great pavilion of the Chief—and she drew back the curtain. Inside, incense burned thick and sweet, clinging to his throat. Three council members knelt in ritual prayer, voices murmuring like wind over water.

When they rose, Tiger Lily's presence filled the room, commanding yet natural, a balance of strength and grace.

Her robe of deep red and brown shimmered with gold thread, catching the glow of the staff she carried—a blue gem pulsing faintly like a heartbeat. Tattoos curled along her neck, glowing softly beneath the skin like living vines.

Her eyes, molten gold, flicked toward Pan, sharp and fathomless.

"The meeting begins," she said, voice silk and steel entwined. The staff's gem flared, casting a spectral map across the stone table.

Pan watched her, not for the words but the rhythm of her movements. Her fingers traced the edges of the island as if it were alive beneath her touch, nails tipped with faint pigment that glimmered with each motion, tethered to the pulse of the land itself.

When she turned to him—"Prince, we ask for your counsel"—her words sounded less like duty, more like confession.

He leaned over the table, their shoulders nearly brushing. "Hook's men are camped here," he said, circling the mark of the cavern. The map's pale blue glow haloed them both.

Tiger Lily's breath caught. She looked at him sidelong, close enough that the faint heat of his presence reached her. "We cannot hunt the forest anymore," she whispered. "And the waters are no safer."

Pan's smile was faint, heavy with knowledge and sorrow. "Then use the danger. Fish along the shallows. Your people have the skill—I've seen it."

The council murmured uncertainty, but her gaze never left his. "If you say it can be done," she whispered, "we will trust you."

The meeting closed in ritual: hands clasped, heads bowed, hearts pounding with unspoken resolve. When the council departed, Tiger Lily lingered, letting the map's glow fade to shadow.

"Come with me," she said softly, voice tremulous yet commanding, an invitation threaded with curiosity.

Pan hesitated, searching her face.

A faint, fierce smile tugged at her lips. "There is something I wish to show you."

Her fingers slipped into his, warm, insistent, and together they walked beneath the rising moon, along the northern edge of the camp—where forest met sea, and the world itself seemed to hold its breath, waiting.

Chapter 9: The Truth

The village seemed to part for them as they walked, Tiger Lily and Pan moving side by side through the flickering torchlight. Shadows leapt across the sand and tents, and the air carried the scent of smoke, salt, and simmering herbs. Women lowered their eyes in silent respect, children peeked from behind woven walls, hands fluttering in tentative waves.

Every gaze that followed them felt heavy, reverent, watching, measuring, whispering in the half-light. To these people, Pan was sacred. To her, he was something less definable—an enigma he himself was still trying to understand.

The sounds of the camp faded behind them, swallowed by the whisper of waves and the cry of gulls overhead. The northern tip of the peninsula stretched ahead, sand curling in a pale crescent against the sea, each grain glinting faintly like powdered glass in the dying light.

Tiger Lily moved ahead, her hair loose, streaming behind her in the wind like molten gold. The setting sun bled along the edges of her tresses, casting the same warm glow across her jaw, her shoulders, the curve of her neck.

Pan followed a few paces behind, mesmerized by the way the light clung to her, softened her features, and caught on the edge of her sharp, noble cheekbones. He thought of the prayers whispered for her heart, the longing that had circled around her like shadows, and wondered—did she know how many had sought what she had never willingly given?

The wind carried the tang of salt and warmth, bristling against their skin. The sea breathed beneath them, an ancient, restless presence, sighing and retreating in an eternal rhythm. Each footstep in the sand whispered: step, step, step—soft, deliberate, finite.

Finally, Tiger Lily spoke, her voice low, deliberate, the kind of voice that seemed to undo spells and open spaces that should have remained shut.

"Do you ever think about the future?"

Pan blinked, startled. He looked to her, then down at the sand around his boots, sinking gently with each step. "All the time," he admitted softly. "Though it isn't the only thing I think about. Why do you ask?"

She slowed, wrapping her arms around herself as the wind tugged at her robe, teasing the edges like fingers of flame. "Because I fear it," she confessed, the words trembling. "The way things are going—Neverland will not survive the winter. My people... they are already hungry."

Her voice broke, raw, fragile. She turned to him, and for the first time in hours, Pan saw her composure fracture. "We almost didn't make it through Hook's last raid."

Golden tears welled in her eyes, catching the last light of the sinking sun. Pan's chest clenched, heart twisting in response. Without thinking, he closed the space between them. His hands found her shoulders, tentative at first, then firm, anchoring her in the world. She let out a sound that was half sob, half breath, and collapsed against him.

They sank together into the sand, knees digging into soft grains, bodies pressed close. Tiger Lily buried her face in his neck, hands clutching at his tunic as if holding on to air itself. Pan held her, feeling her tremors through his arms, the salt of her tears burning slightly against his skin.

He remembered the last time he had seen her break like this—six years past, when grief had driven her to the Hangman's Tree, her sorrow soaking into the roots. They had spoken then of ghosts, of futures stolen by gods who never listened.

Now, her tears slowed, softer, almost silent. When she finally pulled back, she hugged her knees, a small distance away. The space between them hummed with what remained unsaid: grief, yes, but also something quieter, more dangerous, and achingly tender.

Pan lay back, letting the bruised sky stretch above him, shades of violet and blood-orange blending into shadow. Words failed him. His chest ached with thoughts too heavy for sound.

Beside him, Tiger Lily traced symbols into the sand—spirals, flowing waves, runes older than memory. Her voice was soft as twilight: "Tabaldak," she whispered—the name of the god who had shaped her people from wood and wind. Her hands pressed together, then lifted skyward, fingers brushing the dying sun, lips moving in a rhythm older than language.

Pan mirrored her gestures, tracing the same symbols over his thighs, whispering the same ancient prayer. When he finished, Tiger Lily looked at him, wonder softening the lines of her face. "Always so respectful…" she murmured, a ghost of a smile.

The light continued to die, sun sinking low, shadows stretching across their backs like crawling black vines.

Pan exhaled, lying flat again, voice rough against the wind. "I fear that this war... all of this... began because of me."

Tiger Lily turned, eyes wide and luminous. "Pan—"

He did not meet her gaze, staring instead at the bruised horizon. "If I hadn't come here, maybe Hook would never have changed. Maybe Neverland would still be whole." His voice broke, low and aching. "And if I fail now... I fear I'll lose everything—everyone."

For a long moment, she said nothing. Then she knelt beside him, close enough that the warmth of her breath brushed his cheek. "You are the Prince of Neverland," she whispered. "The gods may have cursed you with burdens, but I do not believe they can break you. You will find a way—whether it takes a year or a century."

He turned his head, catching her gaze. Her eyes reflected the last embers of sunlight, golden and molten, and for a heartbeat he almost forgot to breathe.

The tide crept closer, cold and insistent, lapping at their feet. Silence stretched between them, thick with sea salt and sorrow, until the first stars burned through the clouds, fragile points of light in the encroaching night.

Finally, Pan rose, brushing sand from his palms. He reached a hand down to her. She hesitated, then let him take it, fingers warm and grounding. They lingered in that touch, neither moving, as if the world had paused for them.

A hollow, resonant sound split the air—the distant call of a horn from the camp.

Tiger Lily's head snapped toward the forest. Color drained from her face. "No..." she whispered.

Smoke unfurled across the horizon like a living, hungry thing. She broke into a run, bare feet sinking into sand, wind tangling in her hair. Pan followed close behind, heart hammering, legs straining. Screams began, sharp and distant, carried by the wind.

The glow of fire rose over the camp, consuming the night. And in that moment, both knew: whatever fragile peace they had found on the sand, it was already burning.

Chapter 10: The Fight

The camp had become a storm.

Pan and Tiger Lily tore through the panicked crowd, hearts hammering to the rhythm of fleeing feet, the clash of steel, and the war cries that shredded the night. Smoke rolled in thick waves, curling into their lungs, bitter and sharp. The scent of iron — blood and salt — clung to everything, hanging heavy as breath.

Ahead, warriors collided with pirates in a blur of feathers, blades, and bone. Hook's men had come like shadows with teeth, cutting through the forest edge. Their swords flashed in the dying light, jagged reflections dancing across the chaos. Ten men, maybe more, each one moving with brutal purpose, yet sloppy in their overconfidence.

Pan's rapier hissed as he drew it, the polished swept hilt catching the firelight. His muscles moved on instinct, honed, precise. A towering man lunged, dark skin slick with sweat, tattoos curling like serpents across his arms. Their blades met with a shriek of steel, sparks flying, faces inches apart, breaths mingling with the tang of sweat and fear.

Pan twisted, parried, countered — muscles screaming, heart pounding, the world shrinking to the rhythm of attack and defense.

Behind him, Tiger Lily ducked as a woman with quicksilver limbs lunged, dagger flashing in the dim torchlight. Tiger Lily spun aside, hair whipping like a living banner, and grabbed a fallen branch the size of a spear. She gripped it tight, knuckles white, eyes blazing.

Their gazes met across the chaos — Pan's jaw tight, her lips parted — an unspoken oath of survival. Then the storm of battle claimed them again.

The pirates were fierce but undisciplined, relying on fear, speed, and gunpowder. The Clan's warriors moved like flowing water, disarming, binding, turning the tide. Yet the violence was intimate and brutal, spilling into the dirt and mud, soaking the sand with heat and blood.

Pan parried a downward strike, the jolt traveling up his arm. He kicked his opponent square in the chest, sending the man sprawling, then drove his rapier through the back before he could rise. The man's eyes went wide, shock giving way to silence.

A desperate shout cut through the din. "Trey!"

Pan barely had time to turn before another man lunged, sword raised. Blades clashed with grinding force, mud splattering across their boots. The stranger's rage was raw, desperate — the grief of someone who had just watched a brother die. Pan stumbled backward, sword edge grazing his throat.

Tiger Lily saw him falter. Her pulse stuttered. The branch in her hands felt impossibly heavy, but she planted it and swung with precision, striking the attacker aside. Blood streaked her arm where the dagger had nicked her, stinging, but she barely registered it. The woman she fought grinned, tongue flicking over her blade, savoring the taste.

Fury rose like a tide in Tiger Lily — ancient, unstoppable. She swung again, harder. Impact sent her foe sprawling into the dirt, gasping. The Clan's warriors descended, ropes and steel flashing as they bound what remained of Hook's raiding party.

Pan groaned, straining under the weight of another pirate pressing down on him. A boot slammed into the man's ribs, sending him skidding aside. Pan rolled to his feet, breathing ragged, dagger flashing. He flung it — the blade buried itself in the pirate's leg. A scream rose, then was cut off by the hands of two warriors dragging him toward the posts.

Silence fell, thick and shaking, a hush over the carnage.

Pan stood amid the bodies, mud streaking his jaw, blood on his hands. He whispered, barely audible, "Kojh in Mouyo." Rest in peace. The words hovered over the dead like incense, a prayer, not absolution.

But peace was an illusion.

A child's cry pierced the night, raw and terrified. Pan's head snapped toward the sound.

"FOX!"

The name tore from him. In the distance, a boy was dragged by a pirate, knife pressed to his throat. Rage ignited in Pan's veins, hot and bright as magic. He ran.

The forest blurred, wind whipping his hair, branches snapping underfoot. The pirate turned, fumbling for his gun — and Pan's blade was already a streak of silver. One clean cut.

The man screamed, blood fountaining across the sand, arm falling useless. Fox collapsed into Pan's arms, trembling, sobbing into his chest. Pan held him, murmuring wordless comfort, heart hammering.

Tiger Lily was there in an instant, arms around the boy, holding him as if he were glass. Their fingers brushed — warm, trembling, a spark passing between them sharper than any sword.

Pan's attention snapped to the remaining pirate. The air around him shimmered, thin light coiling like mist, eyes glowing faintly gold. Power hummed, coiled tight, dangerous.

The pirate laughed, blood bubbling over his lips. "You're too late," he spat.

Pan frowned, readying himself. Then Tiger Lily's gaze shifted — past him, into the dark trees. Pupils dilated.

"Pan—"

The glint of steel. A whisper of air. An arrow screamed through the night.

Instinct overrode thought. He twisted toward her, arms out, body moving before the mind could catch up. The world slowed, every sense focused on the moment.

Pain erupted across his abdomen like fire. The arrowhead lodged deep, poison biting cold through his veins. His knees buckled. Tiger Lily's scream ripped through the chaos.

Pan yanked the shaft free, blood slicking his fingers. Darkness curled at the edges of his vision, but he searched for her face — needing to see her, needing to know she was safe.

She was — arms wrapped around Fox, expression torn between fury and horror. Pan's lips curved faintly into a smile, breath shaky.

The world tilted. Firelight flared in his vision. Tiger Lily ran toward him, hair wild in the wind, hand outstretched. And then everything went black.

Chapter 11: The Poisoned Light

The forest glowed silver under the moonlight, each tree a shadowed sentinel as they carried Pan back to the village. His body sagged between the warrior's arms, blood streaking the tunic he wore like dark ink. Tiger Lily ran beside them, heart hammering in time with his uneven breaths, lungs sharp with panic.

The metallic tang of blood mingled with the scent of rain-soaked earth, wet leaves clinging to their boots and the hem of their clothes. Her hands, once steady in battle, trembled as they brushed hair from his pale, sweat-slicked forehead. His skin was cold, pulse a faint flicker beneath the surface—but still there. Still him.

"Move!" a warrior barked, pushing the crowd aside as villagers scattered in fear. The healer's tent glowed ahead, lanterns flickering like imprisoned spirits. Tiger Lily shoved the canvas aside and ducked inside, her knees scraping the wet ground.

Lady Rivers was already there—small, hunched, silver hair spilling like threads of smoke. Her eyes, sharp as flint despite age, widened when they saw Pan.

"Poisoned?" she rasped.

Tiger Lily swallowed past the lump in her throat. "An arrow," she said, voice raw. "Dipped in something black."

"Lay him down," the healer commanded. The warrior obeyed, lowering Pan onto the stone slab. His head rolled to the side, and for a heartbeat, his gaze found Tiger Lily's—clouded, but stubborn, refusing to go out.

"Ti…" he murmured, syllables faint, barely carried in the air.

She knelt beside him, gripping his hand before thought could intervene. His skin burned against her palm. "Don't talk," she whispered, voice cracking despite her efforts. "Just... stay."

Lady Rivers moved with practiced, eerie precision—grinding herbs that smelled of earth and storm, pouring water that hissed against hot coals, opening jars reeking of wild roots and lightning.

The air thickened with their scent. She returned to Pan's side, peeling back his blood-soaked shirt. The wound glimmered black-edged, veins already darkening around the puncture. Tiger Lily's throat tightened as her stomach knotted.

"This poison eats through spirit as well as flesh," Lady Rivers said quietly. "It feeds on will."

Pan's jaw clenched as she smeared glowing green salve over the wound. The low, pained sound he made—a growl twisted with gasp—cut into her like a blade. She squeezed his hand, whispering in the old language of her people, words like lullabies from another world, prayers older than memory itself.

When Lady Rivers withdrew, hands wiped clean, she sighed. "Strong-willed, this one. Should've been dead already."

Tiger Lily bowed her head, shoulders trembling as tension bled into exhaustion. The healer's hand touched her arm, warm, grounding.

"He'll live," Lady Rivers said softly. "But the poison will burn for a while. He needs rest… and something to hold onto when the fever dreams come."

Tiger Lily's voice cracked as she nodded. "Thank you."

The old woman's lips curved faintly. "You should rest too, child. Love and guilt share the same weight when carried too long."

Tiger Lily froze, turning away sharply. "It isn't love," she said too quickly. "It's duty."

Lady Rivers' eyes glimmered knowingly. "If you say so."

Outside, mist thickened around the camp, the moon hanging heavy and watchful over the tents. Tiger Lily walked in silence, arms crossed, trying to tether herself. Every breath felt shallow, too small. Every blink conjured the arrow striking Pan, the way his body had arched, his hand reaching for her. Her fault. Her burden.

Fox and the Lost Boys huddled near the firelight, whispering among themselves. When they saw her, the voices fell silent. She bowed her head, lips tight.

"Sleep well, rixj," she murmured.

They replied in unison, palms together. But Fox lingered, eyes wide, glistening with fear and something ancient for a child. She offered a reassuring nod, though her own heart threatened to splinter. Tomorrow, she would speak to him—tomorrow, when her voice did not shake.

Inside her tent, silence pressed close. She collapsed onto the bed, the world swaying around her. Smoke and salt clung to her skin.

She stared at the patch of open sky above, stars flickering like fragile candles in the dark.

"How do I tell Bell..." she whispered to no one.

Her hands moved without thought, retrieving a phoenix-feather quill. She pressed it to her chest for a moment, whispering an incantation:

"Hkunjmekh htij quojjuvo he hto mokjen fte nooxj ih."

The feather ignited, an ember glow reflecting in her wide, exhausted eyes. Words formed in light and smoke, floating above the desk:

Bell, there's been an emergency at the Camp. The Boys are safe, but Pan... Pan is hurt. We need your help, but make sure everyone is home before you come.

She signed it *C.T.L.* The message shimmered briefly, then dissolved into the night like fireflies released into the wind.

Her fingers trembled as she whispered to the darkness, "Don't die on me, Pan."

Back in the healer's tent, Lady Rivers sat beside him. Pan's breath came in ragged, shallow bursts. His lips moved faintly, as if speaking to ghosts. The healer closed her eyes, entering meditation as the veil between worlds thinned. Her spirit drifted into his fevered dreams:

London. Smoke, rain, and the clatter of cobblestones. A boy running barefoot through alleys, chased by a man with a bat and a broken heart.

"Peter!" the man roared.

The boy stumbled, fell, scrambled toward a wall—and the wall swallowed him whole.

When Lady Rivers opened her eyes again, she saw him as he had been, and as he was now:

Pan. Peter. The boy who never escaped fear—only learned to fly above it.

And, beyond the edge of memory, a voice whispered:

"Hey, Peter. I'm James."

Chapter 12: The Memory of Light and Shadow

Lady Rivers drifted through the gauzy layers of dreaming light, gliding along the fragile threads of Pan's memories. Time itself seemed to fold like silk, soft and endless, carrying her to the edge of another world. The air was heavy with gold mist, each breath fragrant with the tang of dawn and the shimmer of forgotten magic. She watched as the boy stumbled through the veil of brick and smoke, slipping from London's narrow alleys into a place where reality wavered and swirled.

He tumbled onto a carpet of soft moss, London's soot and smog dissolving into the first warm fingers of sunlight. Neverland breathed around him—wild, untamed, yet familiar in its strange, dreamlike rhythm. Leaves whispered secrets with the sigh of wind through branches, and the air carried the sweetness of rain before lightning, sharp and alive.

Waiting for him stood a man, tall and steady, more shadow than child, yet full of warmth. Dark hair fell in uneven strands, his skin kissed by sun and salt. His mouth was capable of both mischief and danger, and his eyes held the weary kindness of someone who had seen too much yet refused to surrender to despair.

"Hello, Peter," he said, voice deep and smooth, threaded with quiet danger. "My name's James. A pleasure to meet you."

He offered his hand—not stiff, not formal, but reverent, as though he already understood the weight of the arrival. The boy hesitated, eyes wide, trembling in awe, then reached for him. The touch sparked like fire meeting water, fear meeting warmth, fleeting but anchoring.

James helped him to his feet, palm lingering just a heartbeat too long. "Welcome," he whispered, gaze tracing the impossible horizon where sky and sea shimmered together in impossible color. "...to Neverland."

Peter's lips parted, breath trembling. "Am I...
dead?"

James laughed softly, a sound like wind stirring
through leaves. "No, little one. You're free. Here,
children escape the world's cruel forgetfulness.
Here, you'll never have to grow old, never have
to be afraid again."

Something softened in his expression when
Peter tugged at his shirt. "Are you alright,
mister?"

The simple question fractured something within
James. For a moment, grief shadowed his mouth
before he masked it behind a gentle smile. "I'm
better now that you're here."

He brushed a leaf from Peter's hair with a
reverent touch. "Come. There's something I want
to show you."

They reached the cliff's edge. The world
stretched below them like a jeweled
tapestry—emerald forests veined with gold, seas

glittering like molten glass, the mermaids' faint songs drifting upward with the wind.

"Ready for an adventure?" James asked, hand extended once more.

Peter hesitated a heartbeat before nodding. James' fingers curled around his—warm, calloused, unyielding—and together they leapt.

Wind tore through their hair as they plunged into the sky, Peter clinging to James' chest, heartbeat thundering against his ear. James' laughter spilled over them, wild, untamed, echoing through the limitless air.

"Look," James murmured, brushing a hand through the boy's hair. "Open your eyes, Peter. See the beauty that is yours."

Peter's eyes widened, and the sight stole his breath—endless sky, magic shimmering in every ripple of light, the subtle ache of belonging for the first time.

James smiled, a quiet reverence softening his features. "That's it," he whispered, almost to himself. "You're home."

They landed in a twilight-soaked glade. Before them stood a creature tall and deerlike, coat white as moonlight with streaks of crimson, horns curling like lunar crescents. The world seemed to hold its breath.

Peter stepped forward, captivated. The creature lowered its head, and he pressed his small hand against its snout. A pulse—not of flesh, but of spirit—touched him, binding them in a heartbeat of light.

James watched, stunned. The prophecy whispered among the clans—the child born of pain, carrying the soul of Neverland—manifested before him. Innocence glowed dangerously, and James, once its keeper, found himself trembling with something dangerously close to devotion.

When the creature vanished, James knelt beside Peter, gripping his shoulders. "Son, that was... extraordinary."

Peter's gaze remained distant. "It... spoke to me."

James' thumb brushed the boy's cheek almost without thought. "You're special," he murmured. "More than you know."

Time blurred. Years passed in the fluid reality of Neverland. Peter became Pan—bright, reckless, too wild to belong to anyone. James became the man who raised him yet grew resentful of what he represented: eternal youth while he himself changed, hardened.

They played pirates on the Western Ocean, blades clashing under sunlit waves, laughter echoing across the endless sea. But joy slowly sharpened into longing, longing into jealousy, a silent language neither could name.

Then came the day by the ship's railing: steel flashed, a scream rent the air, a hand severed.

Peter's sword, James' blood—everything they had built fractured in an instant.

Now Lady Rivers witnessed the unraveling: James, older, colder, his hook replacing a hand. His voice thundered through memory, rage and heartbreak intertwining.

"You'll pay for what you did to me, Peter!"

Blades collided—light, shadow, grief, and fury. Pan's eyes burned, sorrow piercing the boyish light within. Hook's laughter followed, wild, tinged with a hollow grief.

"To think the prophecy spoke of you," he sneered. "A savior made of guilt and mercy!"

The dream shattered. Lady Rivers gasped, pulled back into the present, heart hammering as she looked down at Pan. Teal light pulsed across his form, alive, restless—the ghost of love, the ache of power.

She laid a gentle hand on his wound. Light burst free, a storm of color and sorrow rushing outward, filling the tent, spilling into the night like smoke and starlight.

Beneath her touch, his heartbeat fluttered—fragile, defiant.

As his eyes fluttered open, whispering through fevered darkness, a single name escaped his lips, raw and aching:

"Bell..."

Chapter 13: Prince of Pain

Pan stirred awake to a chorus of low chanting—soft, rhythmic, undulating like waves brushing against the hull of some forgotten ship. His lashes fluttered open to a dim, smoke-veiled room. Shadows crawled along the walls, twisting with the flicker of lanterns that hung like captive stars, their light trembling against the haze of incense. The scent of herbs—sweet and bitter—mingled with the faint tang of iron and ash, curling into his nostrils and tugging him further into consciousness.

His breath came shallow. Every limb felt foreign, weighted, as though his spirit had wandered too far and hesitated to return.

And then—her voice.

"Mun," she whispered, the syllable heavy with care, with a gravity that made the air itself still.

Pan blinked. Shapes sharpened. There she was—kneeling beside him, a figure carved of quiet strength. Her hair was threaded with feathers and ash, catching the lantern's glow like bronze caught in dusk. Her skin gleamed softly in the flickering firelight. She moved with the silent precision of someone who had tended wounds that no spell, no sword, could ever fully heal.

"Drink," she murmured, holding a cup to his lips. The rim was cool, the water sharper than he expected. He drank, her fingers brushing his jaw as she steadied him. That fleeting touch ignited a spark through the fog that clung to him like cobwebs.

"How do you feel, Mun?"

Her voice was tender, yet her eyes searched him with the piercing focus of a seer reading omens in shadow. Pan looked at her—the tremor of her breath, the subtle quiver of worry that made her painfully beautiful. "Tired," he breathed, the word fragile, precarious, suspended between them.

She turned, grinding herbs into a paste with measured, deliberate motions, but Pan's voice pulled her back, rough and raw, a sound she had rarely heard from him.

"I'm tired of fighting him, Ti."

The pestle slipped in her hand. He rarely used her name anymore. "I just... I wish it was him you looked up to instead of me."

Her heart stuttered. When she turned, he was sitting upright, swaying, sweat beading on his temples like frost catching fire. His confession lingered, a weight neither could undo.

"Mun..." she whispered, crossing the room, her bracelets singing softly, like rain on stone.

When she reached him, she said nothing. She only took his hand. His fingers twitched weakly before curling around hers—rough against soft skin, desperate, clinging as though he feared she might vanish.

"I'm so tired," he murmured again, voice breaking. "I just want to go back...Before everyone wanted something from me... before Hook... before Fox saw what he saw..."

The name tore something open inside him. Tears welled and fell freely. His body trembled, pressing his palm to his eyes as though he could physically hold back memory and grief. She tightened her hold, grounding him, her heartbeat a rhythm against his.

"Tell me more about Fox," she coaxed, voice gentle, steady.

Pan's chest rose and fell like a drowning man surfacing too fast. His lips parted, ready to speak, but his body gave out. He slumped back, hand sliding from hers, and sleep claimed him again, soft and irresistible.

The light dimmed, curling around them like a sigh. She lingered, thumb tracing the back of his knuckles before rising. His name—Peter—rested silently on her tongue, a secret prayer swallowed by darkness.

By dawn, her prayers were already done. She walked through the mist-laden camp as sunlight bled pale through fog. Children's laughter floated faintly, fragile and thin, competing with cawing crows and rustling leaves.

But not all laughter was whole.

In the corner of a children's tent, Fox sat alone, book open but unread, eyes vacant. The illusions Pan had spun for years had shattered overnight, leaving Neverland unmasked—a place where dream and nightmare tangled.

Tiger Lily's chest constricted. She remembered Pan at that age—restless, wild, desperate to be held, to be believed.

She knelt beside Fox. The hem of her dress brushed his arm; the scent of saltwater and herbs enveloped them, grounding them both. She pointed to the book in his lap—a tale of a black snake that poisoned the earth.

"You know," she murmured softly, "my father once said I looked like this girl."

Fox blinked, corners of his mouth twitching, though the smile never reached his eyes.

She lowered herself fully to the ground, wrapping her arms around his small frame. At first, he stiffened. Then, hesitantly, he melted into her warmth. His shoulders shook with quiet sobs, silent at first, then gradually breaking through.

"I'm afraid," he whispered.

Her hand moved slowly across his back. "What frightens you, child?"

He looked up, eyes glassy, red-rimmed. "I'm afraid of losing Pan... I don't want to lose anyone I love."

The ache in his voice was too old, too vast for one so young. Tiger Lily pressed her lips together, hand moving in slow, reassuring circles.

"Pan will never leave you, Fox," she whispered. "He's bound to this place. To all of us. You'll see."

Fox's breath steadied. Tears cooled on his cheeks.

She began to hum—a low, haunting melody, threading through the walls like a river of memory, echoing the lullabies Pan once sang to calm frightened boys. Fox grew heavy against her shoulder, surrendering to sleep.

"Do you think," he mumbled, half-asleep, "he can teach me to fight?"

Tiger Lily smiled faintly, brushing a strand of hair from his brow. "All you have to do is ask, and he'll never refuse you."

The mist outside lifted, revealing the day anew. But in her heart, the echo of Pan's touch, his voice, his broken confession lingered—a wound that refused to close, delicate and raw, threading through the spaces between hope and loss, love and duty.

Chapter 14: The Whisper of Ash and Light

Back at the Lost Boys' camp, Bell nestled within the hollowed heart of the Hangman Tree. Moonlight bled through the leaves above, silver veins tracing the rough bark, glinting off the edges of knots and scars like the memory of old battles. The boys slept around her, limbs sprawled and unguarded, their soft breaths rising and falling in time with the sigh of the forest. Their dreams wandered wild, untamed, carrying the echoes of children who had never been forced to grow up.

Outside, the air hung unnervingly still. It felt as though Neverland itself held its breath in Pan's absence, waiting for the storm he always carried to return.

Earlier, Bell had overseen the cleansing of their hideout—scrubbing footprints from the mossy floor, scattering leaves to disguise the heartbeats of the camp. From the outside, the Hangman

Tree looked abandoned, centuries untouched. Yet inside, the faint warmth of boyish laughter lingered, like embers waiting to flare.

She sat cross-legged among them, wings folded tight, her glow a soft, dim blue pulse. The forest whispered: distant waves hissed against unseen shores, wind twisted through gnarled branches. The silence gnawed at her. It always did when Pan was gone. He carried life with him—chaos, laughter, danger, firelight—while here there was only the hollow echo of absence.

Bell tilted her head, peering through gaps in the leaves at the black horizon. She longed to take the boys exploring, to soar through the tangled canopy, to feel the rush of wind beneath her wings. But Hook's men crept closer every night, and without Pan, leaving was a gamble they could not afford.

Her eyelids drooped as exhaustion pulled at her, the forest's lullaby creeping through her bones—until—

Crack.

The sharp snap of fire ripped through the stillness. Bell was on her feet before her mind could catch up, wings flaring half-formed. The smell of smoke stung her nose, thick and acrid, climbing with the heat of panic. She burst through the hollow tree, heart hammering like trapped wings. At the top, her fingers found Pan's dagger, still faintly scented with pine, smoke, and the untamable wildness of him.

The treetop opened before her like a black ocean. She scanned the forest, eyes cutting through shadows—but it was the flame that made her gasp. A burst of fire hovered inches from her face, shimmering, folding into itself, taking the shape of a will-o'-wisp. It whispered her name, flickering gold and red like the echo of a heartbeat.

And then the message appeared within the flame—Tiger Lily's urgency burning through the night.

Her breath caught. She didn't need to read twice. She was already running.

"Why does everyone else get to leave but us?" one of the boys asked, rubbing sleep from his eyes. His pout was almost comical against the terror of the night, and it made her heart ache.

Bell smiled softly, brushing a strand of hair from her forehead. Her fingers lingered on his cheek longer than she intended. "Because the world out there," she signed, "is crueler than dreams."

The boy's sigh fell into the still air. Around them, her magic shimmered faintly—warm, melancholy, protective.

She stepped into the night, whispering an old incantation. Blue light rippled along the trunk of the Hangman Tree, suffusing the air with quiet power before fading. Leaves shriveled to gray, lifeless husks. The spell would hide the boys—and the last echoes of Pan's laughter—for as long as she needed.

Taking to the air, her wings protested, weak and aching from disuse. The wind tugged at her, tugging her downward, but she fought it with grit and determination. Every motion reminded her of Pan—his hands steadying her, teasing grin, eyes burning like the edge of a dream she could never fully awaken from.

By the time she reached L'Aura Radieuse, night had settled like a heavy cloak over the camp. Her landing was clumsy; she tumbled through the air, cursing under her breath. A guard rushed forward, lowering his weapon when he recognized the familiar glow of her aura.

"Only you," he sighed, offering a hand. "Come. The Chief waits."

She let herself feel the warmth of his touch, human, grounding, before pulling away.

Inside Tiger Lily's tent, the air was thick with herbs and smoke. Tiger Lily sat beside Fox, who slept fitfully on a woven mat. His aura—once a vibrant, childlike green—was now dim, gray at the edges.

"He saw Pan fall," Tiger Lily whispered, her eyes flickering to Bell. "He saw the blood."

The words sank like stones.

Bell ran a trembling hand through her hair, pulse racing. "Then he's lost faith," she murmured. "When that happens... magic falters."

Tiger Lily nodded. "There's no healing it, is there?"

The silence answered.

Suddenly—

"Bell!"

Tootles barreled through the flap, followed by the others. Their laughter and cries wrapped her in light and chaos, momentarily lifting the oppressive weight from her shoulders.

Then Fox stirred. His eyes flickered open, unfocused, until they landed on her. His breath hitched.

"Bell…"

He stumbled forward, wrapping his arms around her waist, burying his face in her back. His body shook, hot tears seeping through her tunic. Bell froze, wings trembling. Slowly, she cupped his head, holding him gentle and protective, aching.

"I'm here," she whispered, voice like wind through glass.

When he lifted his gaze, there was something fragile and painfully human in it. "I thought you'd gone with him."

"I always come back," she said, though her voice faltered. Sometimes she didn't. Sometimes she longed to vanish entirely.

The other boys clustered around, pressed together like frightened petals. Tiger Lily watched, unreadable, from the corner.

As quiet settled, Bell hummed—a lullaby ancient enough to belong to the bones of the island. The melody wound through the tent, soft and silver, carrying hope through the shadow.

Fox's fingers brushed against her arm. "What if Pan can't fix Neverland this time?"

The chill in the air deepened. All eyes turned to her, pale and anxious, seeking an answer.

Bell managed a fragile smile, though her heart cracked like ice beneath it. "Then," she said softly, "we will remember how to make our own magic."

Her voice trembled as she raised her hands, tracing shimmering patterns in the air.

"Let me tell you a story," she whispered, glow brightening, "a story of when the fairies first learned to love the dark."

The tent filled with light and shadow—twisting, entwined, impossible to tell apart, yet beautiful, a fragile promise in the absence of Pan.

Chapter 15: The Story of Gods and Shadows

Bell slipped her hands into her satchel, drawing them out slowly. Gold dust spiraled up her arms, clinging to her skin like liquid starlight. It shimmered across her slender fingers, catching the breath of every child in the tent. The air tasted faintly of honey and lightning.

Without a word, she raised her hands and the Pixie Dust obeyed—swirling, coalescing, forming an island in miniature before them. The boys gasped as mountains unfurled, rivers pulsed with light, and forests shimmered into existence beneath her touch.

Bell's expression softened—something wistful behind her glowing eyes. Her movements slowed, deliberate, graceful, almost ritualistic. When she spoke, the air itself seemed to listen. The delicate chime of her fae tongue filled the tent like the song of distant glass bells.

Tiger Lily translated softly for the younger ones, though her gaze often drifted back to Bell. The fairy's glow bathed them all in silver warmth, the dust rising around her like a halo of sparks.

"The Gods once roamed the earth
freely,"
 Tiger Lily murmured in time with
Bell's melody,
 "when the land was new and the air
still remembered creation."

Tiny figures appeared, dancing upon the dust-made island—people of light tending to trees, building homes, loving one another under eternal dawn.

"But light cannot exist without its
shadow," Bell chimed.
"And so the Gods began to war."

The island shattered.

Pieces flew like shards of glass across the tent, scattering in bursts of crimson and gold before reforming slowly, tremulous, trembling back into wholeness. The boys leaned forward, their faces lit by fragments of dying starlight.

"They drifted apart," she whispered through Tiger Lily's translation.
"Loneliness crept into their immortal hearts."

"Why?" Binkey's voice was small. "Didn't they have each other?"

Bell smiled faintly—sad, knowing. The glow of the dust flickered across her lips, her cheeks, the soft curve of her jaw. She conjured five figures standing in a circle.

"They stayed near," Tiger Lily said,
"but closeness does not always
mean warmth."

Bell's gaze flicked to the flame-lit ceiling of the tent, remembering another—his grin like wildfire, his touch reckless and soft. She blinked, and the dust in her hands trembled, falling in lazy spirals before reforming again.

"Each God took dominion over their piece of the world," Tiger Lily continued.
"Creation. Destruction. Life. Death. Dreams."

At the last word, Bell's wings twitched—barely visible, but trembling.

She spun her hands, and the Gods birthed humans, smaller and delicate, their bodies luminous but brief. The dust shaped itself into tiny dancers who swirled through the air, their laughter ringing faintly like echoes of joy long gone.

The boys reached out, letting the glowing figures dance across their fingers. For a moment, it felt like innocence.

"But humans grew greedy," Bell sang softly.
"They took what was divine and made it their own."

The light darkened. The air grew heavy. The Pixie Dust turned from gold to scarlet. Now, the little humans bore spears and flames. They chased their creators, their cries sharp as thunder. The tent filled with a dull crimson glow that flickered against every trembling face.

Bell's expression faltered. Her eyes shimmered—not with magic, but with memory. The glow reflected in the wetness gathering there.

Tiger Lily reached over, fingers brushing Bell's shoulder—grounding her. The contact lingered, warm and sure.

> "The Gods cursed the land," Bell
> whispered through trembling lips.
> "They took away its plenty, its joy,
> its color."

The dust dissolved into ash and shadow, swallowing its own light. Crops withered, beasts twisted into monsters. The tent fell silent but for the small sound of Bell's breath.

Two of the younger boys pressed closer to her. "But the humans survived, right?"

Bell smiled faintly, brushing Nibs' hair with the gentleness of a falling feather. "They did. Though not without cost."

Her wings gave a faint hum. "The curse still breathes," she signed. "Even here. Even now."

The boys looked down, subdued. Only Fox's eyes stayed on her—dark, haunted, searching.

> "If even the Gods couldn't live in
> peace," he murmured,
> "how can humans hope to?"

Bell met his gaze. For a heartbeat, the world stilled. There was something raw there—loss, longing, the unspoken ache of children forced too soon into silence.

"I don't think they expected perfection," she said softly. "Only hope."

Fox nodded slowly, but his eyes lingered on her—on the faint tremor of her fingers, the way her breath caught when their eyes met.

The moment stretched, fragile and electric.

Then Bell clapped her hands and the island vanished into dust once more. "We will try again," she signed, her glow flaring brighter. "And when the time comes, we will build something worth their memory."

Tiger Lily rose, tousling Nibs' hair. "Alright, storytime's over. The cooks need help with the feast!"

The boys scattered, laughter flooding the tent again.

But Fox stayed.

He lingered in the quiet, watching her. When the last child disappeared, Bell turned to find him still there—eyes downcast, hands fidgeting.

"Was it true?" he asked softly. "What you said—that Neverland will thrive again?"

Bell tilted her head, then smiled—a soft, secret thing that caught the dim light like a secret flame. She signed slowly, each movement graceful as breath.

> "I said it so you'd believe. Belief is what keeps this world alive."

Fox's expression softened. Then, in a gesture that startled her, he reached out and offered his hand. She hesitated, then placed hers in his. His grip was warm, grounding. He helped her rise, his thumb brushing the inside of her wrist.

A tremor of Pixie Dust slipped from her skin where they touched.

"Thank you," he murmured, bowing his head. His voice was soft, reverent—like a prayer. Then he turned and ran to join the others.

Bell stood there long after he'd gone, her hand still glowing faintly where he had touched it. She pressed it to her chest, closing her eyes as the ache of it bloomed.

When she finally left the tent, the air outside was cool and sharp. The wind curled around her wings like fingers, whispering Pan's name through the trees.

She followed the sound.

Inside the healer's tent, the air was heavy with herbs and smoke. Pan lay still, shadowed by candlelight, his skin pale beneath the sheen of fever. For a long moment, she could only look at him—the curve of his mouth, the faint pulse at his throat, the boy who was never meant to fall.

The healer noticed her and smiled kindly. "He'll wake soon. Go enjoy yourself until then."

Bell hesitated, her wings trembling, torn between duty and the ache that kept her tethered to his bedside. But finally, she nodded.

Outside, the camp buzzed with life—music, laughter, hope stitched together like fragile gold thread. Fox was there among them, smiling again, his laughter light.

Bell's chest loosened. She smiled faintly and joined the others, the scent of fire and feasting curling through her hair, the sound of the forest pulsing like a heartbeat behind it all.

But as she laughed, the wind carried a whisper through the night—soft, half-forgotten, and terribly familiar:

"Bell..."

And her heart stuttered in her chest.

Chapter 16: He's Awake

The festival was in full bloom now — a living, breathing entity that pulsed with heat, light, and sound. The first fingers of dawn bled across the horizon, painting the sky in smears of fire and smoke, a riot of orange and violet bleeding into the deep blue of night's remnants. Lanterns swayed in the humid air, suspended on ropes that crisscrossed the village like veins of light, casting green and gold specters across the packed earth and the rough timber of L'Aura Radieuse. Shadows danced along walls and doorways, folding and unfurling as if the world itself were breathing with the crowd. The drums had been alive for hours, their rhythm raw and primal, echoing off the low hills and the dark, damp trees surrounding the village. Voices — low, guttural, wild — wove around them, rising above the thrum of drums like smoke into the dawn.

Bell sat at the edge of the fire circle, the warmth licking at her bare arms and thighs. She clapped to the beat, her hands catching the firelight, sending sparks reflected in her dark eyes as her laughter tangled with the song of the crowd. Around her, the boys moved like shadows released from chains — newly marked, their faces painted with streaks of black and red, the ceremonial patterns of fledgling warriors. Each step was fierce, sometimes unsteady, alive in a way that made the earth hum beneath their feet. Bell's own paint glistened in the firelight: two red streaks cutting across her cheeks, lined with yellow; a single dot above each brow; eyes circled in black, and a line tracing her bottom lip to her chin — the mark of a full warrior, of belonging.

Every painted face told a story. Of lineage, of victory, of loss, of survival. Tonight was for Pan, yes, but it was also for the ones who remained — for the children and adults who carried his legacy in their sinews and their songs. Every movement, every stomp, every flare of firelight against skin was a heartbeat echoing through the village, a reminder that life persisted despite the darkness that always waited at the edges.

Inside his tent, Pan stirred. Even behind thick canvas walls, the distant thrum of drums reached him, steady and insistent, like a heartbeat calling him back to life. He shifted on the woven mat, wincing as his muscles remembered their weakness, hand going to his temple as he rolled his neck slowly. A groan escaped him — soft, ragged — as he forced himself upright. The healer, Lady Rivers, approached with her usual quiet grace, moving like someone who had seen too much and yet refused to harden, her presence a tether in the storm of memory.

"How are you feeling, Peter?" she asked, her voice low, soft, a thread of warmth in the cool morning air.

Pan blinked, his eyes adjusting to the muted light spilling through the tent flap. He rolled his shoulders, stretching slowly as if testing the integrity of his own bones. "I feel great, htunr-chea." He bowed his head, hands pressed together in respect, a motion learned from years of ritual and survival.

The healer smiled faintly, placing a warm hand on his bare shoulder. Her touch lingered — a moment too long — and he tensed beneath it, a flicker of old instinct.

"You needn't bow to me," she murmured, voice brushing over him like wind through silk. "Today is your day, Mun."

She turned toward the flap, hesitating for a heartbeat as the lantern light outlined her silhouette. "If you feel up to it, there's face paint under the bed. Come when you're ready." She bowed deeply, then slipped into the morning glow, leaving Pan alone with his pulse and the echoes of drums.

He exhaled slowly, running his fingers through his hair, shaking the weight of old ghosts from his shoulders. The memories of battles and loss pressed against him like the ghost of a storm he had never outrun. Shaking his head, dismissing the shadows, he pushed the flap aside and stepped into the thick, incense-laden air of the festival.

The smell of smoke and wild herbs clung to his skin, mingling with the heat radiating from the dancing bodies around the fire circle. His bare feet pressed into the packed earth, warm and slightly damp from the morning mist. Across the flames, he saw Bell — her glow muted against the gold and green of the lanterns, her hair catching firelight, the war paint glinting against her skin like a jewel in shadow.

"Wonder when she got here..." he muttered under his breath.

She noticed him before he could speak. Bell rose gracefully, wings fluttering faintly, and wrapped her arms around him. The scent of smoke and something sweet — wildflowers perhaps — clung to her hair, drifting into his senses, grounding him.

"Peter! How are you feeling?" Her voice was a melody almost swallowed by the drumming and chanting around them, soft and insistent.

He smiled, a faint curve at the corner of his mouth, tired and genuine. "Better than I deserve."

For a heartbeat, neither moved. Then Bell looked away, back to the fire, and his eyes followed her gaze. *Where'd you hide the boys?* he signed silently.

"I used an illusion spell," she signed lightly, though her eyes avoided his. *"The whole tree is hidden. They won't be found."*

Pan's expression hardened for a moment. "Do they know you did this?" he asked softly, a thread of caution weaving through his words.

She shook her head, curling her shoulders inward, a gesture small but unguarded. The way she moved tugged at him in ways he did not wish to name. He stared into the fire, foot tapping against the packed dirt, the heat and light of the flames reflecting in the dark brown of his eyes. The boys were clever, yes, but Hook's men were cleverer still — stronger, more ruthless, relentless. He could do nothing but hope the illusion would hold, hope it would be enough.

Bell's hand found his shoulder then, brushing his skin — light, tentative, grounding.

"I'm sorry," she murmured, voice low, eyes downcast. "I should've asked."

For the first time that night, Pan's smile reached his eyes. "It's fine," he said, warmth threading through the corner of his lips. "Good thinking, actually."

They lingered like that — too close for comfort, too far for confession — until the fire roared higher and the music swallowed them both, weaving them into the pulse of the crowd.

When Pan joined the dance, he moved with the rhythm that came from the core of him — fierce, fluid, unrestrained. His laughter spilled across the circle, bright and clean as if the world could be repaired by sound alone. Across the flames, Bell's gaze followed every movement, her eyes tracing the curve of his shoulders, the flare of his hair in the lantern light, the way his joy seemed to ignite the air around him. Something ached in her chest, a longing she could not name.

Tiger Lily appeared beside her, her own paint streaked with sweat, her chest rising and falling as if she had been running. She collapsed beside Bell, signing lazily, *Pan doesn't seem too happy. Did something happen?*

Bell shook her head, unable to tear her gaze from the fire.

Tiger Lily sighed, tilting her head back toward the early morning sky, the lanterns reflecting in her eyes like distant stars. "If you ever need someone to talk to…" she said softly, voice carrying a weight that Bell understood without words. "You know I'm here."

Bell inclined her head slightly, a quiet acknowledgment, though her thoughts remained pinned to Pan — the way he moved, the way he breathed, the way he carried himself like both a child and a warrior, untamed and whole.

"I just hope," Tiger Lily whispered, "one day we can all dance like this without the fear of war burning at the edge of the forest."

Bell nodded, gaze still fixed on Pan. His laughter was brighter than the firelight, sharper than the lanterns, a light that carried them all for a few fleeting hours beyond worry, beyond danger.

When the dancing ended, the feast began — wild and plentiful. Heaps of roasted fruits, sweet breads, and skewered meats gleamed under the lantern glow. Tiger Lily stood, raising her arms, voice rising in a chant of gratitude and devotion.

"Htunr-chea wek hto zeanhiwap woujh!"

The villagers' voices joined hers, a crescendo of defiance, desire, and devotion. Lanterns reflected in their eyes like trapped stars, the smoke curling upward, intertwining with the gold and green flames. Across the circle, Pan's gaze found Bell's once more.

For a single, suspended moment, the world seemed still. Their eyes met — fire and shadow mirrored, unspoken words humming between them. The drums pulsed again, insistent, pulling them back into the river of movement, laughter, and life.

And as always, the world moved on. Lanterns swayed, fires flickered, and the village of L'Aura Radieuse breathed as one, alive and defiant beneath the early morning sky.

Chapter 17: The Journey Home

Pan and the boys dashed ahead, laughter and shouts tangled in the humid air as the forest blurred around them. Sunlight spilled in molten sheets, burning gold and amber through the canopy, casting the leaves into brilliant shards that shimmered with fire. Every step sent a cascade of shadows and sunlight weaving across trunks and roots, a kaleidoscope of motion that made the boys whoop with delight. Their bare feet barely whispered against the mossy floor, springing from root to root, arms flailing in exhilaration.

A sudden rustle made a few of the younger boys pause, eyes wide as a flash of green-scaled hide darted through the underbrush — a forest sprite, smaller than Pan's hand, but alive with gleaming eyes and delicate wings. They stared, mouths open, before bursting into renewed laughter, racing even faster to catch the boy who had caught their attention only for a heartbeat. Pan's grin was a slash of white against sun-warmed skin, hair tossing behind him like a comet's tail as he led the chase.

Bell moved behind them, her steps lighter than a leaf caught in a gentle wind. Her fingers brushed over bark, ferns, and brambles, the faint hum of her magic threading through the air, leaving a shimmer that whispered of protective wards and subtle illusions. Her gaze traced the boys as they tumbled and spun, tugging Pan into games of chase that seemed to bend the laws of gravity.

One of the boys seized her hand, small but insistent, pulling her into their path. Bell stumbled lightly, caught by their momentum, and allowed herself to be drawn alongside Pan. His gaze flicked to her, a subtle, almost imperceptible spark crossing the space between them. Her fingers grazed his in a fleeting touch — soft, electric — and for a heartbeat, Pan's chest thrummed with a rhythm that echoed the distant drumbeats still lingering in the air from the festival's end.

"Looks like they want to play with you now," he murmured, voice low, intimate, a silk thread tying him to her. Bell smiled, warm and unguarded, letting her eyes sweep over the chaotic orbits of the boys, their laughter spilling like liquid light through the forest.

For a while, Pan hung back, watching. The children's joy drew Bell into their orbit, her movements fluid and unrestrained, hair catching the final glimmers of the sun, tipped with firelight. Her laughter, like bells carried on the wind, tugged at something deep inside him — a longing he refused to name, a tension coiled like a spring. He remembered the rhythm of her wings, the soft brush of her fingers, the impossible lightness with which she carried herself.

Then came the distant crackle. A tremor in the air. Bell stiffened instantly, chest tightening, senses prickling like static across her skin. Pan's head snapped toward the sound, eyes narrowing, muscles coiling like a predator's. The boys paused mid-step, sensing the tension, and

Pan shot Bell a quick, sharp glance — a silent exchange laden with unspoken understanding. She nodded once, barely perceptible, and he dipped his head, slipping into the shadows of the forest with the grace of a shadow itself.

The cliff came swiftly, a sheer drop into the valley below, where smoke and fire tangled with the golden light of the setting sun. The scent of burning wood and earth assaulted him, thick and acrid, biting into his lungs. Below, the forest seemed alive with chaos, flames devouring the underbrush and scattering villagers and creatures alike. Hook's men moved among them like shadows, black and insidious, consuming every glint of light with calculated menace.

Pan's body tensed. Fists struck the earth, sending small jets of green flame curling into the sky — a silent roar of power, furious, untamed. But then, as though the forest itself conspired against him, a numbness seeped in, curling around his limbs. He rose, yet floated above himself, powerless, green flames expanding outward in silent fury without anchoring to his will. His mind screamed against the phantom weight pressing down, but his body refused command.

Behind him, Bell faltered. The illusion surrounding the Hangman's tree strained at her, threads of magic flickering as fatigue clung to her like a heavy cloak. Her own attention had been elsewhere — on warding the children, on hiding the boys from sight — but the sudden void in Pan's aura drew her focus like a tethered kite snapping loose. Her chest tightened, limbs trembling, a tremor of magic and fear coiling inside her.

"Pan," she called softly, voice threading through the invisible cord that linked them. It carried across space, light and sound bent to her will. "You need to relax."

He obeyed, though unwillingly. The pit beneath him, dark and viscous like tar, seemed to hold his body as she guided him through the trance. "I don't know what's happening, Bell..." he admitted, voice ragged, stripped bare of its usual defiance and humor.

She knelt nearby, hands hovering as if she could pierce the ether itself and anchor him to the world. Her voice carried a melody that cracked the armor around him — part command, part lullaby. "It happens to the best of us, Pan. Just breathe… clear your mind."

Slowly, painfully, he felt the sensation return. Fingers, arms, heart — one by one, the feeling returned, raw and electric. He collapsed into a seated position, sweat and ash clinging to his skin, lungs burning as he drew in deep, shuddering breaths.

Bell waved at the boys to slow their pace. Fox, small and keen-eyed even in exhaustion, fell back, hand brushing against hers. His young face was etched with worry, lines far too heavy for one so small. She offered a fleeting smile, dipping her head slightly, but the weight of the morning's exertion drew her down, and she sank onto a moss-covered rock.

The moment came too quickly. Her energy faltered with a soft, electric pop — a disruption in the air that set the hairs on Pan's arms upright. Bell slumped forward, weight falling lightly into Fox's arms. Her chest pressed against him, almost deliberately, and he inhaled a breath heavy with her scent — wildflowers, smoke, and an indefinable something that made his chest ache with unspoken longing.

Pan stumbled through the brush, still recovering from his surge of power, and froze when he saw her cradled by the boys. His pulse constricted in his chest. With urgent grace, he pushed through brambles and low-hanging branches, reaching her in seconds that felt like eternities. His hands found her body, lifting her with ease, her weight settling against him — soft, trusting, and alarming in its intimacy.

"Is she...?" one of the boys squeaked, tugging at Pan's sleeve.

"She's fine," Pan murmured, voice low, protective. The way he adjusted her in his arms lingered in the air, intimate, tethered, deliberate. "Just tired. Let's keep her safe."

Bell's hand drifted unconsciously, brushing against his chest. Pan's fingers twitched at the touch, a thrill running through him. Words hovered on the edge of lips neither dared to speak: confessions of fear, desire, and the fragile ache that had been simmering between them for years.

They moved in quiet synchronicity through the Soultaur tunnels, shadows stretching and twisting around them, the boys scattered but safe. Laughter faded into the distance, replaced by the damp, earthy scent of the tunnels. Pan's eyes never left Bell's; hers, in turn, found his when courage allowed. A slow, dangerous intimacy wove itself through the space between heartbeats and shadow, stronger than words could capture.

At last, the quiet settled around them, thick with magic, fear, and the faint hum of lingering adrenaline. Neither spoke, neither needed to. In the hush of the forest, beneath the weight of power and peril, a silent promise hung between them: neither would let the other fall, not here, not now — and perhaps, someday, they might finally speak aloud the words that their hearts had been screaming from the start.

Every rustle of leaves, every whisper of wind through the tunnels, every distant echo of flames or creature movement held them together. The forest seemed to acknowledge the tether, holding its breath in a reverent hush. Pan's heartbeat, ragged from exertion, aligned with the faint pulse of Bell's wings, the electric warmth that thrummed through her magic, her care, her presence. They were both more than flesh and bone in this moment — they were light and shadow, flame and ember, chaos contained within the fragile human forms they occupied.

As they finally emerged from the tunnels, the forest opening above them into dappled shafts of sunlight, the boys' laughter resumed, fragile and jubilant. Pan's arms cradled Bell as she leaned slightly into him, their breaths mingling, the shared rhythm of heartbeats, wind, and life stitching them back together. For a fleeting moment, everything else — Hook, danger, the lingering scars of battles — fell away.

In that quiet, suspended space between motion and stillness, Pan realized the depth of his need to protect her, and Bell recognized the fragility of the man before her — brilliant, unyielding, but vulnerable beneath the armor of defiance. For all the chaos, all the peril, they were tethered — not by obligation, not by duty, but by the raw, impossible gravity of connection.

Chapter 18: The Lost Boys

When they finally reached the Hangman's Tree, the devastation spread before them like a silent warning. Broken branches jutted from the earth at odd angles, splintered wood scattered across the mossy floor, and leaves lay strewn like ash, their edges curled and browned from scorch and storm.

Shattered scraps of metal glinted faintly in the waning sunlight, catching his eye with every movement — twisted remnants of traps, hooks, and armor discarded in haste or anger. The air was thick with the acrid scent of smoke and burnt undergrowth, a bitter perfume that clung to hair and skin, to clothes and lungs alike.

Pan and the boys remained pressed low in a thick bush just beyond the edge of the wreckage. Their breaths were shallow, each exhale a careful hush against the tension in the forest. Pan's eyes swept over the ruined canopy, the ground, and the shattered remnants of their home, tracking the subtle sway of shadows, the movement of leaves, the distant flicker of firelight lingering like a warning.

He whistled softly, a tune carried from childhood — a lullaby his mother had hummed through endless nights, smoothing nightmares into silence. The melody was a fragile balm, threading through the forest, calming not just the boys but himself, weaving quiet into the chaotic aftermath around them.

Bell stirred at his side, fragile as a bird, eyelids fluttering in the dim light, chest rising and falling with shallow breaths. Pan eased her to the ground with careful hands, the strength of his fingers enough to ground her, not to startle. "You're home now… rest," he murmured, the words heavy with relief and something unspoken. His hand lingered a moment on her shoulder, warm against the chill of the evening. Her gaze met his, sharp yet soft, and in that instant, the space between them thickened, charged — silent, intimate, weighted with the things neither dared to voice.

The boys clustered near them, small bodies huddled together like a living shield around their friends. Voices trembled, but Tootles' soft smile offered a quiet assurance.

"It's alright... Bell just needs to sleep," he said gently.

His words, careful and warm, threaded through the tension, drawing the boys into a sense of purpose. They helped Pan carry her inside, murmuring encouragement like a chorus of soft prayers, treating her presence as if it were the hearth of their home — the center around which everything else orbited.

Once Bell was settled on the bed, Pan stepped back, brushing imaginary dust from his hands, though the pulse of his heart kept drumming in his ears, the memory of her weight against him lingering like fire on skin.

The room smelled of herbs, damp moss, and faint smoke — a scent that clung to every surface, threading through the draped fabrics and wood beams like a memory of survival.

Outside, the boys moved with a strange combination of urgency and reverence, clearing debris and collecting broken metal and splintered branches. Pan's gaze returned again and again to Bell's closed door, an ache tightening in his chest like a knot of living shadow. The forest around the Hangman's Tree seemed to sigh under the weight of the evening, whispering secrets through rustling leaves and the soft creak of bending boughs.

Pan moved through the wreckage, hands gathering what could be saved, pausing only when Thomas approached, boots crunching softly over scattered twigs and ash. Pan rested a hand lightly on the older boy's shoulder, a gesture of grounding in the chaos, a silent acknowledgment of trust and responsibility.

"Thanks for looking after them... especially after Bell left," he murmured, voice low, threaded with gratitude that words barely contained.

Thomas nodded, stooping to pick up a particularly jagged shard of metal. "Anytime, Prince," he replied, his voice calm but steady, eyes not leaving Pan's for the briefest moment — a shared understanding of the delicate balance they all walked.

The evening thickened like smoke settling between the branches. Pan moved quietly through the forest's shadows, preparing food for the boys. His hands worked with habitual precision, chopping roots and herbs, kindling the small fire to a controlled warmth.

The smell of cooking mingled with the damp earth, with the lingering smoke of ruin, creating a strange comfort. All the while, his thoughts drifted inexorably to Bell — her small frame, fierce yet fragile, a shield, the impossible balance she held between fragility and indomitable will.

The boys ate with the reckless appetite of survivors, chewing and swallowing in hurried bites, their chatter punctuated by occasional laughter that sounded brittle, like glass under pressure. Afterward, they cleaned, their young hands scrubbed and brushed with care, before tumbling into sleep.

Pan remained, patrolling the area, ears straining to catch the slightest whisper of movement among the shadows. The night pressed around him, thick with secrets, heavy with the scent of pine and smoke, and alive with whispers only he could almost hear — the murmurs of the forest itself, the ghosts of memory and warning woven into the wind.

Then, a flicker of light drew his gaze — soft, tentative, almost shy. Before he could investigate further, Bell appeared at the railing, her silhouette delicate against the darkened expanse of the night. She was tired, yet upright, as though each step required an internal argument with exhaustion itself.

Pan hurried to her, hands gentle as they guided her, careful of her weariness. *"You work too much,"* she murmured, leaning her head lightly on the railing, eyes closed as though to shut the world away.

He chuckled softly, shaking his head, the sound blending with the rustle of leaves and the distant hum of nocturnal life. "Says the one falling asleep while standing..."

Her eyes flickered open, catching his gaze, and the world seemed to narrow around them. The forest, the distant rustle of night creatures, the faint glimmer of firelight — all faded, leaving only the hush of their shared space.

"You know what I mean," she signed, rolling her eyes, her frame thick with fatigue and something more, a tremor of vulnerability she rarely allowed herself to reveal.

He crossed his arms, leaning casually against the railing, though the weight of his concern shimmered faintly in the aura that glowed around him, green and restless, echoing the tension in his chest.

"I know... but if I don't, who will?" His voice was firm yet unguarded, eyes never leaving hers, seeking truth in the vulnerability she showed him.

Bell's fingers twitched, brushing almost imperceptibly against his arm. The touch was a whisper, fleeting, but magnetic, igniting a warmth in Pan's chest that coiled tight, dangerous and undeniable. The moment stretched, delicate and suspended, heavy with all the confessions neither dared to speak.

Finally, Pan moved closer, taking her effortlessly into his arms. The intimacy of the gesture was grounding, protective, yet charged with an unspoken electricity that made the space between them hum. He carried her back inside the tree, navigating the narrow wooden steps with ease, settling her gently upon the bed.

His lips brushed her forehead — a fleeting, reverent touch. Bell's eyelids fluttered closed, a soft sigh escaping her lips as though exhaling the exhaustion of the world. Pan lingered, thumb tracing the curve of her cheek, feeling the fragile, dangerous weight of the connection between them. Every heartbeat, every breath, was a reminder of the intimacy and the peril of the emotions they shared but dared not name.

When he finally stepped back, the room seemed emptier, the air charged, thick with what had just passed between them. His eyes flicked to the boys' sleeping forms, then back to Bell's resting figure, and a sharp ache twisted in his chest. In that silence, suspended between duty, danger, and desire, Pan recognized something he had long tried to deny: this quiet, fragile moment was not just a respite, but a beginning — a tether, a promise, a spark that neither could ignore.

Outside, the wind whispered through the forest, carrying the scent of damp earth, crushed leaves, and faint smoke from distant fires. The canopy above shivered with movement, the stars peeking through gaps like distant eyes, watching, patient, knowing.

Within the Hangman's Tree, the firelight flickered across the walls, casting dancing shadows that seemed to echo the heartbeat of the room, of the moment, of everything Pan and Bell were too afraid to name aloud.

He allowed himself one last glance at her, committing the sight to memory: small, fragile, impossibly alive in the quiet after chaos. The steady rise and fall of her chest, the relaxed curl of her fingers against the sheets, the way even in exhaustion she seemed untouchable yet desperately human.

Then Pan turned, stepping softly toward the window, letting the quiet night fold around him. Each step was a rhythm, a tether back to the forest outside, to the boys who slept with dreams untouched by fear, to the fragile home they were rebuilding from the wreckage. And in the deep hush, beneath the green glow of his aura and the soft pulse of life all around, Pan understood — some moments were too fragile to speak, too precious to waste on words. Some moments were meant only to be felt, to be remembered, until the world allowed them to be spoken aloud.

Chapter 19: The Discovery

Pan spent the night in the watchtower, perched above the forest like a sentinel suspended between earth and sky. The wind whispered through the leaves far below, carrying hints of smoke from last night's fire and the subtle tang of damp moss clinging to the trees.

The moon hung low, a pale sentinel in the sky, and its silver light glinted off the edges of his map, illuminating the careful markings and secret paths he had etched over countless nights. Every dotted line, every spiral and cross, was a lifeline — a way to reclaim what Hook had taken, to gather reinforcements, and to defend Mermaid Lagoon before Neverland slipped further into shadow.

He traced a finger along a route through the forest, imagining the movements of Hook's men, the flutter of his boys ahead, the wind brushing their hair and the thrill in their laughter. Each detail demanded attention: where the trees leaned low enough to hide a quick escape, where the cliffs rose sharply, where the tide would mask footprints on the sand. His jaw tightened with focus, green eyes catching the faint gleam of dew on the underbrush in his mental projection.

By dawn, the first fingers of sunlight filtered through the treetops, dappling the clearing below with molten gold. The boys began to stir, their small forms stretching and yawning, clinging to the wisps of dreams that still lingered in their sleep-heavy minds.

Pan had already been working for hours, the tables set, breakfast prepared, each detail executed with mechanical precision but infused with care. Plates of Poyuta pancakes, stacked and steaming, awaited them, drizzled with berry syrup that glistened like garnet in the morning light. He saved the last portion for Bell, mindful of her exhaustion, the quiet vulnerability she had shown the night before weighing on him even now.

The first boy to emerge yawned widely, hair tousled and damp with dew, eyes still clouded with sleep. Pan's smile spread across his face, bright and almost boyish, and he planted his hands on his hips with exaggerated enthusiasm.

"Who's ready to get started with today?!"

His voice carried across the clearing, trying to ignite the same spark of excitement in the boys that burned in his own chest, even as worry gnawed at the edges of his thoughts.

Laughter erupted in response. Plates in hand, the boys dashed toward him, sunlight catching on their hair and clothes, scattering across the clearing like ribbons of energy. Pan watched them with a rare ease, noting the gleam of excitement in their eyes, the small gestures of camaraderie and mischief.

He saw Fox's careful steps as he balanced his plate, the way Tootles' grin threatened to split his face entirely, and the wide-eyed wonder of the youngest boys as they savored each bite, laughter spilling from them like sunlight through leaves.

Pan allowed himself a moment of quiet pride, but the comfort was fleeting. When he stepped into the foodshed for a garoni, his thoughts drifted inevitably to Bell. He imagined her small, tired form as she had appeared the night before, the soft curve of her cheek against her arm, the quiet tremor in her breath. Even now, her presence lingered in the air — a ghost of warmth and fragility that made his pulse thrum with a tension he didn't dare name.

Thomas lingered over the map, scowling as though it were a living thing trying to thwart him.

"You're making plans for the invasion already?" His voice was sharp, edged with frustration, but beneath it ran an unspoken concern that mirrored Pan's own unease.

Pan met his gaze, shoulders straight, jaw set. "Yep," he replied. "We don't have a choice, Tom."

He knew the words sounded stern, but his green eyes softened when they flicked toward the window, where Bell's sleeping form remained peaceful and unaware of the world outside. A pang of something unnameable twisted in his chest.

Thomas slammed his fist against the table. "Untrained kids, Pan! You plan to send them into a war they barely understand?"

His tone was both accusation and plea, as though he were attempting to shield the boys from the weight of what Pan already carried.

Pan rubbed a hand down his face, exhaling slowly through his nose, the tension coiling in his chest like a snake.

"No, Thomas. I'll tell them everything before it comes to that. I promise." The words were firm, but they carried the tremor of someone who had seen the stakes, who had stared too long into the darkness to ignore the cost.

The air itself seemed to hum, taut with unspoken fears, frayed at the edges by the sheer anticipation of the coming battle. The morning sunlight touched the clearing in gold, scattering across the boys' hair, over the rough wood of the tables, over the scattered tools and scraps of past skirmishes. Then, a small voice broke through the tension — hesitant, innocent, trembling like a leaf in the wind.

"Why are we fighting someone?" A younger boy's eyes were wide, pale in the early light, and his voice carried the fragile weight of genuine fear.

Pan knelt slowly, meeting the boy's gaze, lowering himself so that the height between them was gone. His hand hovered over the child's shoulder, hesitant, protective, though the boy flinched slightly, as if sensing the storm behind Pan's calm exterior. His heart tightened, a pang he knew well — the echo of Bell's quiet vulnerability the night before.

"You're right," he murmured softly, voice low, warm. "We're preparing for a big fight. But it's to protect everyone... all of Neverland." His aura shimmered faintly, a green pulse catching the morning light as though the forest itself acknowledged the gravity of his words.

The other boys gathered, questions tumbling out like a chaotic storm. Fear, confusion, anger, and curiosity collided in their voices, each one a thread pulling at the fabric of his resolve. Pan's eyes flicked toward Thomas for guidance, but the older boy had disappeared into the fray, leaving him unmoored amidst a sea of voices, each one a reminder of the fragility of their lives and their innocence.

A flutter of wings interrupted the chaos — delicate, urgent. Bell, roused by the noise, hovered at the window, her small frame outlined by the early sun. Her wings shimmered like fractured glass, catching light and scattering it in splinters across the clearing. She landed lightly, eyes scanning the gathering below, and Pan felt that familiar tug in his chest — the mixture of fear, awe, and something deeper, unspoken.

He longed to reach for her, to take her hand and steady both her and himself, but the crowd of boys pressed around him. Instead, he lingered at the edge of the commotion, memorizing the way light caught her hair, the curve of her jaw, the faint furrow of her brow. The forest, the clearing, the morning — all faded around her presence, leaving only the almost unbearable tension of near-confession, of a connection neither dared to acknowledge aloud.

Bell's gaze met his, flickering with understanding, worry, and something tender that hovered between them. Pan's fingers twitched, itching to brush a loose strand of hair from her face, to close the gap, but the boys' clamoring kept him rooted. He carried that quiet ache with him, a steady thrum in his chest, through every instruction, every plan, every fleeting glance.

He watched as she moved among the boys, tending quietly to their needs, adjusting their clothes, calming the frightened, her motions efficient yet gentle, imbued with a lightness that seemed almost unnatural after the night's terrors.

She was small but unyielding, tired but still brimming with energy reserved for others, not herself. The sight brought both pride and a sharp ache to Pan's chest, a reminder of everything he had to protect, and everyone he could not fail.

The morning unfolded in layers of sunlight and shadow. Pan's mind alternated between strategy and silent observation, plotting paths, calculating risks, imagining ambushes, all while keeping one green-gold eye on Bell.

He noted how her wings caught stray beams of sunlight, how her hair shimmered with copper highlights, how the faintest tension in her shoulders spoke volumes of her weariness and determination. Even as the boys asked questions, complained, or laughed, she moved like the axis around which their fragile world spun.

At one point, a younger boy stumbled, almost dropping his plate of breakfast. Bell reached out with the speed of instinct, steadying him, her small hands firm and certain. Pan's pulse quickened as he watched, the urge to step in nearly irresistible. He forced himself to remain behind, knowing the tension of the morning required him to balance both leadership and restraint, strategy and presence.

The sun climbed higher, turning dew to mist, shadows to gold. Pan's shoulders loosened slightly as the rhythm of activity carried forward — the boys ate, the maps were examined, plans murmured among them. Yet through it all, the undercurrent of something unspoken persisted: the quiet ache, the tether of worry and desire that pulled him toward Bell, that made every glance, every shared breath between them, feel vital and dangerous.

By the time the boys finished their breakfast, Pan allowed himself a brief exhale, leaning against the watchtower railing, letting the wind catch his hair, letting the weight of responsibility settle across his shoulders. Bell hovered nearby, wings brushing the air with delicate ripples, her gaze meeting his for the briefest heartbeat.

And in that suspended moment, amidst the chatter, the planning, the tension of an approaching storm, the connection between them held — fragile, electric, and unyielding, a quiet truth that would follow them into every battle yet to come.

Some battles, Pan realized, were not fought with swords or spells. Some were fought in heartbeats, in glances, in the quiet spaces between the chaos — and he had never been more aware of that truth than he was now.

Chapter 20: The Plan

Bell leaned at the sill and watched the boys gather like a tide around Pan. The illusion that had softened the edges of their world was thinning—its gold fraying at the seams—and with it came questions the boys had never thought to ask. If the glamour fell entirely, Pan could stop pouring every scrap of his will into keeping the lie alive. Maybe then the surges would ease. Maybe then he could fight with clearer hands.

She dropped from the window and drifted through the crowd, wings folding tight so as not to startle them. The boys parted as she moved—part respect, part fear, part the simple hush that lived between them whenever she spoke. She reached Pan and seized his shoulder. The touch was firm; a bell of authority rang in her voice.

"What is the meaning of all this?" she quickly signed, and the forest stilled to listen.

A shout answered, raw as a wound. "Pan's been hiding things from us for years!"

The accusation blossomed into a chorus—anger, betrayal, fear—voices like a swarm. Bell's jaw tightened. She set her hand flat on the table at Pan's elbow, letting her presence spill warmth into him.

"He hid things to protect you," she signed, and the words were more plea than rebuke. *"Everything he did—every illusion, every lie—was to keep you safe and keep Neverland whole."*

For a long moment the din dwindled. It didn't erase doubt, but it planted something steadier in the air: a thread of trust. Pan took that thread and tugged. He climbed onto the table and drew the crowd close, Bell lifting beside him at his side. Up there, his silhouette was a thin thing against the brightening sky, and the boys' faces, upturned, looked like lanterns waiting to be lit.

"I know you have questions," he said, voice lower than the drums that still pulsed somewhere down by the village. "And I'll answer them—honestly." He hesitated only a breath, and in that sliver of quiet his eyes found Bell's.

Her fingers rested at his wrist, a small, grounding weight. He swallowed. "I used illusions because I wished someone had wrapped me in one when I was your age," he admitted, and the admission—soft, ragged—dropped through the crowd like rain. The boys shifted; anger frayed into something pained, then curious.

He told them, simply, of the man who had turned Neverland greedy and cruel; told them the truth of Hook's raids and of the hollow lagoon. The words were blunt as knives, but Pan put them through his own throat first. Bell watched him watch the boys, and her chest ached with a tenderness so fierce it made her wings hurt. When he faltered, she tightened her grip on his sleeve. He drew breath and went on.

A small voice cut through—Ace, bright-eyed and earnest, stepping forward as if to walk straight into a storm without fear. "Pan cares about us," he said, plainly. "He's our leader."

The other boys echoed him; the sound broke the tension like dawn splitting night. Pan's shoulders slackened; the dangerous, brittle humor that had been his armor cracked and fell away. He smiled—not the careless grin he showed the world, but something private, fragile.

"Thank you, Ace," he breathed. "Now," Pan said, voice steel returning, "I need you to help save Neverland."

He spread a map across the table—creases like old scars—and tapped a place on the northern coast. "In three days, we storm Mermaid Lagoon. We take back the prisoners and the magic they've bled dry. The warriors will do the fighting; you will hold the pockets, lead the people to safety afterward. It will be dangerous. It will be ugly. But it is necessary."

Questions rose like smoke; Pan answered where he could, promising honesty about everything he'd hidden. When one boy asked, timidly, "Will you come back?"

Pan's mouth tightened. He wanted to say more—things that had nothing to do with strategy: that he feared losing them, that he feared losing Bell—but instead he met Bell's eyes and nodded once, hard.

"I will come back," he said. The vow hung between them heavier than any blade.

After the others dispersed, Bell slipped into the tree to find Pan's folders—hundreds of pages of scratched ink, maps smelling of smoke and salt, plans drawn in a dozen handwritings across years. She gathered them into her arms; the papers nearly eclipsed her small frame.

When she returned, Pan reached out to take them. Their fingers met over the stack—callused hand, tiny, dust-flecked one—and something electric ran up both their arms. Pixie dust leapt from her skin where their palms touched, a soft glittering that made the air taste like rain.

"Thanks," Pan murmured, voice rough.

He held her gaze a fraction of a second too long, and there was an honest hunger in it that had nothing to do with strategy. Up close, she could see the exhaustion pooled under his eyes, the green smudge of magic that never quite left his skin. He lifted the papers and held them like an offering.

She stepped nearer, the space between them thinning until their breaths mixed.

"Be careful," she signed—no one would have called it advice. More like a plea, threaded with something fragile and raw. Her fingers brushed his knuckle; the pressure there was small, deliberate. Pan's thumb found her wrist and squeezed, a simple anchoring that spoke of debt and of more.

"I will," he promised. The words were private, meant only for her.

He spread the map again and showed the boys the plan: diversion on the east, the chains that bound the prisoners exploited at low tide, a narrow inlet where the Lagoon's watchers were weakest. Hands raised, questions asked, strategies sharpened like spears.

Still, beneath the mechanics of warfare, the air between Pan and Bell thrummed—soft touches, the way they leaned toward one another when he worked a knot free of paper, the way her shoulder brushed his when she shifted a map. It was small: an ember shy of flame, but hot enough that both knew the burn was coming.

When at last the meeting broke and the boys scattered to pack and prepare, Pan lingered. The clearing emptied until only the two of them remained—lantern light and their breathing. He walked to her and stood too close to be casual.

"Thank you," he said again, and this time his voice was close enough that she felt the breath warm along her face.

She lifted her chin. "You'd do the same for me," she replied, but the answer sounded less like certainty and more like confession. They both smiled, small and raw. For a heartbeat, neither moved.

Then Pan reached out and tucked a stray hair behind her ear, fingers resting for an eternal second at her temple.

"Stay with me," he said—no command, no plan—only a wish exposed to the night. His voice trembled at the edges.

Bell's wings fluttered, and she let herself fall into his hand, into the safety his palm promised. *"Always,"* she whispered—half vow, half sacrament.

They stood there a while, two silhouettes beneath the boughs, the map of Neverland folded between them like fate. Around them, the boys' laughter echoed off the trees, oblivious and necessary. The war waited like a maw beyond the lagoon, but for that thin, stolen instant, they were not leaders or soldiers; they

were two broken things finding a shape that
might hold them both.

Chapter 21: Our Promise

After Pan debriefed the boys, they all got started on their preparations for their raid into Mermaid Lagoon. He had some of the smaller boys building weapons while others trained. Pan had to finish marking up the map so that he could share the plan with all who wished to join him. He sat alone in his room which now sat at the top of the tree, he continued to stare at a map he'd looked at for years already.

He flopped onto his back as he looked out the window, watching as most of the boys prepared for the next few days. Though he noticed that a few of the boys sat to the side, talking amongst themselves. He wondered if they were speaking of leaving the lost boys, while he wouldn't hold anything against them, it would be heartbreaking if they did leave.

While Pan never showed it, he had gone through so much loss and heartbreak over the years and he didn't need more. Though with the bomb he just dropped on these children, he'd understand if they decided to ultimately leave and go on their own paths. Maybe they'd even start their own Lost Boys or begin their own lives.

He sighed softly as he looked back towards the map, which was now in the hands of Fox, who was looking it over.

"Why look at the same old boring map if you already have a solid route in and out of Mermaid Lagoon?"

Fox looked back up towards Pan as he fluffed the map in his hands. Pan sighed softly and looked to the side, looking at the back of the map.

"Well we shouldn't have one solid route in and out, we could encounter anything when we go out there..." Pan pointed at the back of the map, creating a lump for Fox to see.

"There's been a lot of activity out there lately, but a few weeks back it was deserted land..." Fox looked at the lump on the map curiously. He nodded and looked around the map curiously.

He pointed on the map where the mountains connected to Mermaid Lagoon.

"What about if we went through here, while it's rough terrain, I don't think that they'd see us coming and we could have an advantage."

Pan looked at Fox confused and then tore the map out of his hand, carefully placing it on the table.

He looked over the spot where the mountains met Mermaid Lagoon and it was almost perfect. Pan nodded and looked at Fox before leaning back, crossing his arms as he thought for a moment.

"This would be good, but if Hooks ship points in this direction, we would be spotted if anything went wrong."

Fox nodded and looked at the map. "Yeah and you have it marked off because of that, but as soon as Hook sees the army of children and Indian warriors running towards him, he'll know we're there anyway..."

He slapped his hand on the table, pointing at the mountains. "I believe this is our best shot at winning Mermaid Lagoon back..."

He sighed softly before nodding looking at the map. He took his pen and circled the mountains.

"If we go through with this, we'll have an advantage, it's close to food and water so that some of us can camp out..." He scoffed and looked to the side, towards the boys.

"But we could be seen by Hook and the entire plan could go down in flames?"

Fox sighed and looked at Pan, placing his hand on Pan's shoulder. "It's a good plan, so good that you thought of it and doubted it..."

Pan chuckled softly and looked up towards Fox, his smile fading softly as he placed his hand on Fox's shoulder, their arms against one another.

"You know, you're a great kid and I'm sorry that your life on Earth didn't pan out..." He sighed softly, before embracing Fox in a hug.

"Thanks for the idea, War Chief" Pan pulled away from Fox and ruffled his hair. Fox chuckled softly, swatting at Pan's hand before punching Pan's shoulder.

"Now go join the boys in training, or you could pack some bags of food and water, maybe pack some of the weapons?"

They both had a laugh before they calmed down, Pan started cleaning up as Fox made his way back down to the boys. He stood in the hallway as tears flooded his view, Fox chuckled softly through the tears.

"Why now..."

He wiped his nose and looked to the side, towards Bell who was looking for Pan. Bell made eye contact with Fox, a look of worry spread on her face as she ran over to Fox. She met him on the ground, embracing him. He sobbed into Bell's arms as they sat on the ground.

"Want to tell me what's wrong?" Bell signed as she pulled back, meeting Fox's gaze.

Fox shook his head and looked to the side, wiping the tears from his face. "It's nothing, just a little overwhelmed I guess..."

He sighed and looked down at the floor as he thought to himself. He didn't know the emotions he felt but they were overwhelming and they took up every space of his imagination. Bell sighed softly and looked at Fox, helping him up as he calmed down. Bell smiled softly and gave Fox a giant hug, Pan walked out, looking between the two of them confused.

"*Are you both good?*" Bell looked at Pan and nodded, smiling brightly.

"He told me about the plan you two came up with for the rebellion."

Fox looked at Bell confused and then nodded, looking back towards Pan.

"Yep, I might even tell everyone before you get to it Pan"

Fox laughed and saluted as he walked down to the rest of the boys. Pan smiled softly before looking back towards Bell, who looked towards Fox with a melancholic look on her face. Pan nudged her and smiled softly, looking towards Fox.

"Pixie Dust for your thoughts?" Bell chuckled softly and pushed Pan playfully. Pan laughed softly before leaning towards Bell, she sighed and looked up towards Pan.

"He was feeling overwhelmed, that's all, I'm sure most of the boys are..."

Pan nodded and looked to the side before thinking for a moment.

"So how'd you know he came up with the plan?" Bell looked at him confused before shaking her head as she walked around in a circle before standing in front of him.

"Well, you went in there to continue planning, and he went in there when you did that so I just assumed..." Bell shrugged and smiled brightly, shimmering almost. Pan shook his head and brought her in for a hug.

"You are amazing Bell, thank you for sticking around for all this time..." He smiled softly and looked towards the boys. Bell smiled softly, patting Pan on the back.

"I intend to keep the promise I made to you all those years back...cause a-"

Pan smiled softly and shook his head, joining in with Bell as she spoke.

"*Cause a fairy always keeps their word no matter what...*" Bell smiled brightly and nodded, before fluttering off to help the boys. Pan chuckled, shaking his head as he made his way out to the boys. He remembers the day he made his promise with Bell like it was yesterday. They made it when Pan was a kid and it was a time when Hook was still around.

"*While memories last forever and never die, the truest of friends stick together and only say goodbye at the very end.*"

Chapter 22: The Night of Our Promise

The night air was thick with the brine of the sea and the acrid tang of smoke, a bitter reminder of Hook's cruelty. Every breath Pan drew carried the weight of charred wood, scorched earth, and the memories of the camp—Tiger Lily's father had his grief etched into the sand, the laughter of the boys now silenced, the lives burned away leaving nothing but ash and sorrow. The waves lapped at his boots, curling around his ankles like icy fingers, each pulse of water a cold echo of the storm of guilt and helplessness roiling inside him. The horizon was a smudge of darkness, indistinguishable from the shadow that pressed upon his chest. Even the moon seemed reluctant to shine, hidden behind clouds heavy with the salt of the sea.

Pan's gaze wandered across the desolate shoreline, to the blackened remnants of tents and the skeletal forms of half-burned trees. Every flicker of flame, every wisp of smoke, haunted him, drawing his thoughts into the past—the frantic scrambling of the boys, the terror in Fox's eyes, the moment when Bell had faltered, and the sharp, bitter ache of near-loss that had lodged itself deep within him. He swallowed against the lump in his throat, feeling the familiar sting of helplessness that never truly left him.

A soft glow appeared at his side. Tinkerbell. Her wings trembled slightly, scattering flecks of golden light into the darkness like sparks from a dying fire. She did not speak at first, allowing him to drown in the ache of memory, to feel the weight of failure pressing down like a stone. The gentle rhythm of the waves provided a hollow accompaniment, their ceaseless push and pull echoing the turmoil in his chest.

Finally, her voice broke the silence, soft, hesitant, a thread of warmth weaving through the cold night.

"You can't carry all of it alone."

Pan turned, and for a moment the relentless weight of leadership, of vengeance, of all the duties and horrors he had borne, slipped into something more fragile. The green of his eyes met the golden shimmer of hers, and in that instant, he saw not a fairy, not a comrade, but a reflection of the vulnerability he rarely allowed himself to show.

Without thinking, he reached out, brushing a stray strand of hair from her face. His fingers lingered, tracing the curve of her cheek with the gentleness of someone who feared the world would shatter if he let go. The contact sent a shiver through him, a quiet ignition that burned hotter than any anger, brighter than any fire.

"I don't... I don't know what to do without you, Bell," he admitted, his voice low, roughened by exhaustion and emotion, almost breaking under the weight of the truth. It was a confession he had never allowed himself before, a crack in the armor that he wore as tightly as his own skin.

Her tiny hand found his, clasping it with surprising strength. It was a lifeline, a tether in the storm.

"Then don't," she whispered, the heat of her touch searing through the chill of night. *"Stay. Stay with me, with my people. Don't let this darkness consume you."*

Pan's chest tightened, the air between them charged with something both urgent and fragile. He knelt slightly, lowering himself to meet her gaze fully, letting the moonlight, the spray of the sea, and the shadows of the ruined camp wash over them both. The curves of her face, the tremor in her wings, the way her light flickered with unspoken fear and unyielding resolve—all of it struck him with the force of a revelation.

"I promise," he murmured, his thumb brushing over the back of her hand, tracing the delicate curve of her wrist. The words were soft, tentative, but carried the weight of an oath, heavy and impossible to ignore.

Bell's wings fluttered nervously, her glow brightening as she leaned closer. Their foreheads met lightly, almost a whisper of a kiss, a tether of warmth in a world that had grown too dark, too cold. She exhaled against him, a breath trembling with the unspoken, and whispered, *"And I'll be here, Pan. Always. Even in the shadows you can't yet see."*

For a long moment, they simply existed in each other's presence, hands entwined, breaths mingling with the salt air, the sound of the waves, and the faint crackle of distant fires. The echoes of the destroyed camp seemed to fade, absorbed by the vastness of the night, leaving only the quiet, fragile heartbeat of their connection.

Pan's mind wandered briefly, imagining the camp as it had been before — the boys' laughter ringing across the tents, the firelight dancing on Bell's wings, the smell of fresh fruit and herbs drifting through the night. Those memories were sharp and sweet, and then bitter, reminders of what had been taken and what must still be protected. He shivered, the wind curling around him, tugging at his cloak, brushing sand against his skin like tiny reminders of his vulnerability.

Bell's glow intensified, bathing them both in soft, golden light. The warmth pressed against the cool salt of the night, a tangible proof of her presence, of her promise. Pan felt the pulse of her heartbeat against his palm, a rhythm that anchored him, steadying him as he had so often steadied the boys. And in that pulse, in that shared moment of fragile intimacy, he recognized the depth of what he felt — a bond that went beyond loyalty, beyond companionship, a tether of hearts intertwined against a world determined to break them.

"Even if we lose everything else," Pan murmured, voice hoarse, "we still have this. We still have each other."

Bell's wings quivered, light spilling like liquid gold around them. *"And I will never let go,"* she said softly, her lips almost brushing his forehead in a fleeting, deliberate touch. *"Never. Not as long as I live."*

The wind picked up, carrying with it the scent of salt, smoke, and the faint sweetness of the flowers that still stubbornly bloomed along the cliffs. Pan closed his eyes, letting the sound of the waves and the rush of the air drown out everything else—the destruction, the pain, the looming threat of Hook. For a few heartbeats, there was only this: the warmth of Bell's hand in his, the gentle press of her forehead against his, the quiet assurance of unspoken promises.

Pan finally released her hand, though reluctantly, letting it linger a moment longer before withdrawing, leaving behind a ghost of warmth. Bell hovered beside him, a soft glow in the darkness, wings flickering as though resisting the night itself. He watched her, memorizing the curve of her jaw, the tilt of her shoulders, the way the light caught her hair. Even in exhaustion, she radiated resilience, courage, and a beauty that burned brighter than any flame Hook could set.

He breathed in, tasting the salt and smoke, grounding himself in the moment, knowing that the battles ahead would demand every ounce of strength he possessed. But for now, he allowed himself to simply exist in her presence, to let the night and the sea and the silence cradle them both.

The waves continued their relentless push and pull, each crash against the shore a reminder of the world's persistent rhythm, indifferent to their grief and loss. Yet, within that rhythm, there was a strange comfort — a promise that even amidst destruction, some constants remained. Pan clung to that promise like a lifeline, as tangible and necessary as Bell's small hand in his.

"Tomorrow," he whispered, almost to himself, "we will fight. We reclaim what's ours. But tonight..." His gaze met hers again, searching for the courage reflected in the shimmer of her wings, the unwavering strength in her eyes. "...tonight, we just... exist. Together."

Bell's glow softened, settling around them both like a protective veil. *"Together,"* she echoed, her voice a fragile echo against the roar of the waves.

They lingered there, their foreheads pressed together, hands intertwined, hearts beating in sync with the eternal pulse of the sea. The night stretched, a tapestry of darkness and gold, shadow and light, grief and hope interwoven so tightly that to pull on one thread would unravel them all. Yet neither moved, neither spoke, as if even breathing too loudly might shatter the fragile world they had created in that moment.

Time blurred. The stars wheeled overhead, indifferent witnesses to their quiet vow. Pan's mind wandered, imagining every future battle, every peril they might face, and he realized that no sword, no spell, no plan could match the gravity of this bond. It was the thing that would anchor him when the world tilted into chaos, the tether that would draw him back when he felt himself slipping into despair.

And when, at last, the waves began to retreat slightly, leaving the sand smooth and cold beneath their feet, Pan allowed himself a small smile, faint but real. Bell mirrored it, her wings fluttering once, twice, then folding against her back as she hovered lightly. The glow around her softened, no longer urgent, a steady luminescence that promised both warmth and protection.

Pan turned to face the horizon once more, the first hints of dawn brushing the edges of the sky with pale gold. The fires Hook had left still smoked in the distance, but in that fragile, electric moment between night and day, between despair and hope, Pan understood something he had not allowed himself to feel before: he was not alone. Not now. Not ever.

And whatever battles awaited them—Hook's wrath, the fires, the treacheries of Neverland—they would face them together. Not merely as leader and ally, but as hearts tethered in a fragile, unspoken covenant, bound by trust, devotion, and a love that had yet to find its

words but already carried the weight of
everything that mattered.

Chapter 23: Together

In that quiet, salt-scented night, with the waves lapping around their feet and the ghost of the camp fading behind them, Pan and Bell stood in the hush that followed their confession. The sea shimmered silver under the moon, and for once, there was no laughter, no games - just breath and heartbeat and the heavy pull between them.

Bell's wings flickered faintly, like embers about to catch. *"So that's it, then,"* she said softly. *"No leaving, Not ever."*

Pan's voice was rougher than she'd ever heard it. "Not unless death drags us apart."

The words hung between them, and something in him broke - or maybe it was something that finally healed. He stepped closer, his hand finding her face as though it had always known the way. Her skin was cool from the sea air, and when he brushed his thumb along her cheek, her glow trembled beneath his touch.

She looked up at him, eyes wide, luminous.

"Pan..."

"Don't," he whispered. "If you say my name like that again, I'll forget every rule I ever made."

Bells's lips parted, a breath caught between laughter and longing. *"Maybe that's the point."*

And then he kissed her.

It wasn't the mischievous, careless sort of kiss Pan might give after a victory. It was slow - careful at first, as though he were afraid she might vanish if he pressed too hard. But when she pulled away, the kiss deepened, and the world seemed to tilt. The sea hissed around them' her glow spilled over his skin, tracing gold where his hands slid to her waist.

She rose on her toes, fingers tangling in his hair, and he let out a quiet sound - half a groan, half a sigh. For a heartbeat, they were only warmth and pulse, the wild ache of something new and inevitable.

When they finally broke apart, Bell's wings fluttered wildly, throwing flecks of light across the sand. *"You're shaking,"* she whispered.

"So are you," he breathed, forehead resting against hers. "Maybe that's what forever feels like."

She smiled - soft, dizzy, undone. *"Then I'll take it."*

He drew her in again, his lips brushing her collarbone, his hands tracing the outline of her back. The night seemed to tighten around them, the tide pulling closer, the air thick with everything unsaid-

CRASH!

A sudden clatter erupted from the camp. Shouts, laughter, and the unmistakable sound of something - or someone - breaking.

Pan froze, eyes narrowing. "The boys," he muttered darkly.

Bell's glow flickered between irritation and amusement. *"They've always got terrible timing."*

He exhaled, a crooked grin tugging at his lips. "Always."

She leaned in, whispering against his mouth, *"This isn't finished."*

"Never is," he murmured back. And with one last look - that wild, unspoken promise still burning between them - he turned toward the noise.

Chapter 24: You Ready?

The halls of the Hangman Tree hummed with quiet, determined activity, a low chorus of hammering and carving that echoed faintly against the hollowed wooden walls. The air was thick with sawdust, the metallic tang of sharpened blades, and the faint perfume of the forest that seeped through cracks in the bark. Lanterns swung from carved hooks, their flickering flames casting long, wavering shadows that danced across the boys' focused faces. Each spark of light caught the edges of tools and weapons, the rough-hewn timber of improvised shields, and the raw determination etched into the young warriors' brows.

Tinkerbell flitted through the hall like a shard of moonlight, her tiny glow illuminating the wooden planks beneath her as if the darkness itself recoiled from her presence. Her wings shimmered in faint pulses, casting prismatic fragments against the walls and highlighting the sharp concentration on the boys' faces. She leaned close to a younger boy, guiding his trembling hands over the components of a miniature pistol. The boy's jaw tightened, eyes wide with frustration, as the pieces refused to fit, but Bell's soft murmurs of encouragement—so low that only he could hear them—slowly coaxed steadiness into his motions. Her fingers brushed his repeatedly, each touch sparking the faintest shimmer of fairy light along his hands, as though magic itself lent strength to his fumbling fingers.

Pan lingered in the doorway, observing quietly. The weight of the coming battle pressed against him like a physical force, a tightening coil of responsibility and dread. He could feel the pulse of Neverland itself in the marrow of his bones, the wild, untamed heartbeat of the island thrumming in tandem with his own. Every snapped twig in the shadowed corners of the hall, every nervous glance from the boys, seemed amplified in his mind. His chest tightened as he watched Bell, the familiar ache settling like molten lead at the center of his being. She was small and fierce, luminous against the dim hall, and in her gentle guidance of the boys, he saw not only devotion but a quiet, radiant power that left him raw with admiration—and longing.

Fox moved silently among the boys as well, a stabilizing presence in the chaos. His hands were steady, adjusting grips, testing balance, nodding with approval. When he glanced at Pan, a soft smile tugged at his lips—a subtle promise, unspoken, of loyalty and trust. Pan's heart constricted unexpectedly, a warm pull he had almost forgotten existed, one that tethered him in ways beyond strategy or duty. He had spent years moving through life unanchored, and the sudden realization that Fox's steadfast presence could ground him shook him more than any threat Hook might conjure.

Pan shook his head, forcing himself back into focus. The satchel in his hands was heavy with the meager rations they had managed to gather: dried fruit, scraps of bread, small hunks of preserved meat. Every ounce felt like a statement of hope, a promise that they would endure. Fox leaned against the doorway, arms crossed, watching him, eyes wary yet unwavering.

"I'm coming with you," Fox said, voice teasing at first, but the sharp edge of concern betrayed him. "Someone needs to keep the Prince of Neverland safe."

Pan's hand found Fox's shoulder instinctively. Their eyes met, and for a heartbeat, the world narrowed to just them: the heat of shared responsibility, the electric awareness of proximity, the quiet acknowledgment of reliance. Pan leaned in slightly, pressing his forehead against Fox's. The hall seemed to dim around them, the hammering and murmurs fading to a distant murmur.

"Together till the end, Peter," Fox whispered, wrapping Pan in a tight embrace that left warmth lingering in its wake. Pan chuckled softly, patting his shoulder, reluctant to pull away, feeling the dangerous comfort of the boy he had come to care for deeply. Even amidst the threat of Hook's forces, the intimacy of this small moment—the mutual recognition of dependence, of trust—was grounding.

"Now come on," Pan murmured, voice low. "Let's get you a weapon and get moving." His hand lingered on Fox's shoulders as they walked together through the hall, a tether neither of them dared break. The soft swish of Bell's wings behind them, the muted clatter of tools and weapons, and the faint scent of sawdust and forest combined into a pulse that seemed to bind the three of them together in unspoken resolve.

Meanwhile, Bell hovered among the younger boys, moving like a shard of moonlight over the wood and stone. Her tiny hands brushed against theirs, a spark of magic threading through the air with each touch, igniting focus and determination. One boy trembled, gripping a pile of sticks that refused to cooperate. "They won't stay together..." he muttered in frustration, his voice a sharp, anxious note against the low hum of the hall.

Bell knelt beside him, their hands overlapping. She murmured softly, a gentle incantation, and tiny green firefly lights began to swirl around them, illuminating her face in soft emerald glow. Her wings twitched as if resonating with the magic, and the boy's hands, now steady under her guidance, began to obey. Pan watched from a distance, chest tightening at the sight. The quiet power of her touch, the patience in her gestures, the calm she exuded even in the thick of impending war—everything about her made him ache in ways he could not name, in ways he had long forbidden himself to feel.

"Ready?" she whispered to the boy, her hands going back to his. When he nodded, she smiled—a smile that held encouragement, light, and a whisper of mischief. It was the kind of smile that made Pan want to cross the hall in one movement, to reach her and lose himself in the glow she carried, even as the shadow of Hook's threat loomed over them.

Later, as the warriors of La Clan de L'Aura Radieuse gathered, tension coiled through the air like a living thing. Pan's presence was felt even from afar; his strategic mind spun through possibilities and contingencies even as his chest tightened with the weight of responsibility. Bell, sensing the shift, pulled Tiger Lily aside, her glow flickering faintly in the dim, firelit hall.

"How is Pan holding up?" Tiger Lily asked, voice low, laced with concern. Her hands were steady, but her eyes betrayed the unease she felt.

Bell's gaze drifted toward the distant mountains, picturing Pan and Fox moving through the shadows of the forest. Her glow pulsed softly, and she spoke with a quiet tremor, *"I… I'm afraid he's going to get himself killed if he isn't careful."* Her voice was almost swallowed by the ambient hum of preparation, but the weight behind it was unmistakable.

Tiger Lily's hand found hers, fingers curling around in a gentle, grounding squeeze. "Aren't we all afraid of that?"

Bell smiled faintly, the worry in her eyes softened by the contact. *"I guess... that's why I'm here. To help."* The words hung between them, a quiet acknowledgment of shared responsibility and mutual trust. Their hands lingered together, threads of warmth and devotion weaving a fragile, unspoken promise.

She turned her gaze toward the horizon, where Pan's figure moved alongside Fox, shadows stretching behind them in the early morning light. Her words carried on the wind to anyone who might listen—or perhaps just to the universe itself. *"Let's bring everyone home."*

Her words were meant for more than the Lost Boys; they were meant for Pan. They were a reminder, a tether of light threading through the gathering darkness of Neverland, a signal that even in the face of encroaching danger, there was a bond stronger than fear. That bond was more than friendship—it was loyalty, devotion, and a quiet, fierce insistence on survival and unity.

Pan's figure halted briefly, hearing the faint echo of her words in the wind. He felt the weight of them settle into his chest, grounding him amidst the whirl of strategy and impending violence. Each careful step, each deliberate motion toward readiness, was bolstered by the knowledge that Bell's light—and her presence—would follow him, a quiet beacon amid the chaos.

As the boys tested their weapons, hammered and carved, and sharpened their swords and knives, the hall seemed to pulse with a life of its own. The lanterns flickered against Bell's glow, casting shifting patterns on the walls and floor, mimicking the nervous, tentative energy of those within. Every strike of hammer against metal, every whispered incantation, every careful adjustment carried a weight beyond the physical task; it was an investment in survival, in hope, in a future they all clung to tenuously.

Pan moved among them, checking grips, steadying hands, and offering the occasional encouraging word. His gaze frequently drifted to Bell, hovering just above the wooden planks, radiant in her own fierce diligence. Every brush of her wings, every tiny flick of her fingers, seemed to imbue the boys' efforts with invisible strength. His chest tightened, a mix of awe and longing twisting through him. He had faced countless dangers, countless battles—but the quiet intensity of her devotion, her patient care, struck a chord within him that rivaled any victory or defeat.

Even Fox, standing by the doorway, seemed drawn into the spell of the hall's energy. His presence was steady, grounding Pan's own shifting emotions, yet Pan felt the undercurrent of warmth and loyalty—an unspoken tether that bound them together through trust, responsibility, and something closer to the heart than either dared name.

As the sun began to rise, spilling gold across the forest beyond the tree's walls, the boys finally paused, hands raw, eyes shining with fatigue and pride. Bell hovered above, wings tired but glowing brighter for a moment in triumph, her gaze sweeping over the gathered warriors. Pan's heart swelled at the sight, a taut knot of pride, fear, and longing.

He knew that the battles to come would test them all—faith, courage, loyalty—but in this moment, surrounded by light, determination, and the flickering magic of Bell's presence, he allowed himself the rarest of reprieves: hope. Not the reckless hope of ignorance, but the tempered, glowing, unwavering hope that even in the darkest night, there could be a tether of light strong enough to pull them all through.

And as Bell whispered once more to Tiger Lily, her words carried on the morning breeze like a promise: *"Let's bring everyone home."*

Pan felt them as a vow, a covenant, a bond that tethered his heart to hers, and for the first time that day, he believed they might—just might—survive what was coming, together.

Chapter 25: The Trek

The forest beyond the Hangman's Tree had grown quiet, the usual rustle of leaves and distant cries of Neverland's creatures muted by the looming storm. Tinkerbell's glow flickered faintly in the distance, hovering over the younger boys as they adjusted their weapons. Even from afar, Pan could almost feel her presence—a warmth brushing at the back of his neck, a spark of reassurance in the shadowed air. Her glow seemed to cling to him in the edges of his vision, an invisible tether pulling at his attention, reminding him of her tiny, insistent heart guiding theirs.

His mind wavered between the immediate threat below and the small, tender moments she had offered earlier: her hands brushing his in fleeting gestures of care, her voice soft yet commanding as she taught the boys to steady their grips, and the faint shimmer of magic that always lingered closest to him, a quiet reassurance that he was never truly alone. Even now, he felt it, as if a fragment of her had slipped into his bones, keeping him steady against the storm-wrapped world.

Fox trudged alongside him, the weight of the Pisu strapped across his shoulders making his gait awkward and heavy. "These things are too damn heavy," he muttered, voice tight with effort, shoulders straining against the rough packs.

Pan chuckled softly, the sound swallowed by the low rumble of thunder above. "We can't rely on Bell for everything," he said, voice low, carrying a strange intimacy in the quiet between them. "Even fairies get tired. And when she's gone... it's on us."

Fox's hand brushed against his as they adjusted their packs, a fleeting contact that made Pan's chest tighten in a way he couldn't—or wouldn't—name. He glanced down at Fox, whose eyes were bright and earnest, shadows of anxiety and determination woven in their depths. The storm mirrored the tension coiling in Pan's gut—an excitement laced with fear, and beneath that, something sharper, hotter, almost unbearable in its intensity.

The wind tugged at their hair and clothes as they climbed higher, the rocky path slick beneath their boots, yet neither spoke much more than necessary. Every footfall seemed amplified, every shift in balance a reminder that the coming battle was no longer a distant rumor but a creeping inevitability.

When they reached the ledge of the mountain, Pan set the Pisu down carefully, letting his fingers linger a moment too long on Fox's shoulder. The touch was deliberate in its gentleness, a silent acknowledgment of trust and shared stakes. "After this is over," he murmured, leaning slightly closer so their arms brushed together, "you'll figure out a better way to carry our hunts. I trust you for that."

Fox's smile was slow, teasing, but the blush creeping across his cheeks betrayed the playfulness he'd hid beneath the surface. "I'll do my best, Pan," he said, voice husky, and there was something lighter than the hunt in it, a reminder of their journal relationship that made Pan's chest both swell and constrict at once.

Pan allowed himself a heartbeat to glance toward where Bell might be, imagining her hovering just beyond sight, tiny hands resting on his chest, her glow radiating warmth against the darkening storm sky. He shivered, part from the chill wind that whipped along the cliff, part from the memory of her close presence—the delicate touch of her fingers, the pulse of her magic reaching him before anyone else, the way her small frame seemed to anchor him even amid chaos.

Below them, Mermaid Lagoon stretched across the valley like a sheet of liquid obsidian, the storm rolling in from the sea, dark clouds swallowing the pale morning light. Waves curled and hissed against the jagged rocks, foam sparkling faintly in the half-light, and the figures moving across the beach were indistinct, but Pan could see them: Hook's men swarming, moving like black ants across sand and stone. Lightning tore through the clouds, jagged and blinding, illuminating the water and the enemy alike in brief, white-hot flashes. Pan's fingers itched for his weapons—not just the Pisu in their packs, but the knives and bows strapped to his back—but also for something else, something impossibly small yet vital: a hand to hold, a touch to anchor him in the whirlwind of danger.

And then Hook's figure appeared, impossibly composed, standing in the crow's nest like a black silhouette against the fractured sky, violin in hand. Pan froze, heart hammering as if it could fracture his chest. Hook's gaze locked onto him, piercing through the distance, as if he could read the very depths of Pan's soul. A dark, intimate smirk tugged at the corner of Hook's mouth—a challenge not just to his skill or courage, but to the raw, tangled emotions Pan barely allowed himself to recognize. For a heartbeat, the world narrowed to the two of them: predator and prey, leader and oppressor, and the storm above mirrored the tempest in Pan's mind.

Fox's voice broke the spell, grounding him. "Let's go before we get stuck in the rain." His hand brushed Pan's again as he shifted the satchel, fleeting contact that nonetheless sent a spark up Pan's arm, making the hair on the back of his neck lift.

Pan exhaled slowly, letting the tension unwind just enough to keep his footing. He turned toward the trail leading back to Hangman's Tree, the mountains behind them shrouded in mist, the forest swallowing shadows and light alike. He carried more than Pisu that day—anticipation, longing, and a gnawing fear that Bell, watching from afar, could sense everything he carried and yet would not voice it.

Even as they walked, the storm rolling behind them like a living thing, Pan's thoughts lingered on his smirk, on the chill it brought in the face of oncoming battle, on the bond tethering him and her together, fragile yet unbreakable. No battle, no army, no Hook could touch that. But the pull of it, the ache of it, the dangerous closeness that hummed between him, and Bell, was almost unbearable.

Rain began to fall in sparse, cold droplets, tapping against the leaves and slick rocks, soaking the moss beneath their feet. Pan's boots slipped in the mud, each step a reminder of the precarious balance between danger and survival. Yet he moved with a kind of urgent grace, muscle memory and instinct carrying him forward even as his mind drifted to Bell: the small, stubborn defiance in her eyes, the way her glow brightened when the boys accomplished something she had taught them, the quiet, unspoken warmth she offered him that no one else could.

Fox stumbled slightly, catching his shoulder instinctively, and Pan held out a hand, steadying the young warrior. The shared effort, the electric awareness of touch in the pouring rain—it was a dangerous intimacy neither dared acknowledge but both felt like a current running beneath the surface.

They paused briefly on a high ridge, the wind whipping around them, rain slicing in stinging needles. Pan let his gaze sweep across the valley below, taking in the chaos of Hook's encampment and the roiling waves beyond. Lightning split the sky, illuminating Hook once more in the crow's nest, violin poised as though mocking their vigilance. Pan's green aura flared faintly, tinged with fury, anticipation, and the ghost of longing, a pulse that reached even Fox.

Fox leaned in slightly, his voice a whisper and yet steady despite the storm. "You've got this, Pan. We've got this." His eyes glimmered with unshed fear, loyalty, and something that seemed almost like devotion—but Pan couldn't linger on it, not yet. He nodded once, sharply, swallowing down the thrum in his chest that came from more than adrenaline.

As they descended the trail toward Hangman's Tree, the forest around them alive with wind, rain, and the scent of wet earth, Pan's mind refused to leave Bell. He imagined her hovering above the treetops, wings catching the faintest light, her tiny hands reaching for him, her voice soft and commanding as she orchestrated the younger boys below. The thought was a tether he clung to, a quiet strength amid the chaos threatening to tear Neverland apart.

Every step, every brush of hands, every shared glance between him and Fox carried weight beyond the physical journey. They carried the weight of Neverland's fate, of Hook's looming menace, and of a fragile, dangerous intimacy threaded through every moment. Even the storm seemed to sense it, winds whipping through the branches like a chorus attuned to unspoken emotions.

By the time they reached the sheltering canopy of the tree, soaked to the bone and streaked with mud, Pan allowed himself one more glance toward the horizon. Bell's glow lingered faintly in memory, a promise of light, warmth, and connection, a reminder that even in the darkest storm, some bonds could not be broken.

The rain fell harder, soaking them to the skin, and the distant thunder rolled like the drumbeat of fate itself—but Pan felt anchored, not just by duty, but by the quiet, unspoken ties between hearts too close to ignore. It was fragile, electric, and terrifying—but it was theirs, and it would carry them into the chaos awaiting below.

Chapter 26: The Problem

The crow's nest creaked with every gust of wind, the timbers slick beneath Hook's fingers as he leaned back, chest pressed against the mast, eyes scanning the storm-laden horizon. Clouds coiled and twisted across the sky like serpents, black and silver under the fractured light, moving with a slow, deliberate menace.

The wind tore through the rigging, singing across the sails, and the faint metallic clash of the distant ore-mining operation reached his ears, a rhythmic percussion against the soft hum of his men singing their work songs. Their voices rose and fell, blending with the groan of wood and the hiss of rain against the hull, clashing with the metallic scraping below as the prisoners broke stone and twisted metal alike, each striking a testament to the crushing inevitability of Hook's plans.

Hook's fingers drifted absently to the tattered photograph in the pocket of his coat. The paper was frayed, edges curling with age, the image of

Pan mid-leap frozen in time: hair tousled by the wind, eyes bright, about to land squarely on Hook's chest in one of their rare, sunlit days of fragile camaraderie.

Even after decades, Hook could still feel the thrill of that instant—the electricity of it, the pulse of life that only Pan seemed capable of stirring in him. A subtle, dangerous warmth coiled in his chest as he stared at it, half nostalgia, half something darker, sharper.

A distant glimmer of movement across the mountains caught his eye, the faint sheen of Pisu horns reflected in the flashes of lightning tearing the sky apart. Hook's pulse tightened, a thrill of anticipation winding through his veins, and for a moment, time seemed to compress.

Pan's gaze met him across the distance, sharp and unyielding, and the faintest spark—almost imperceptible—rattled Hook like lightning striking the mast. His lips curved into a slow, calculated grin as the first drops of rain began to fall, tiny percussion against the tension threading the valley below, a storm within a storm, unspoken and undeniable.

Pan shifted the Pisu on his shoulders, adjusting the weight with careful precision, raindrops plastering his damp hair to his forehead. Fox trudged beside him, smaller but no less determined, cheeks flushed from exertion, brow furrowed under the low, rolling clouds. "So, our spot on the mountain is brilliant, right?" Fox asked, voice bright despite the oppressive gray around them, a grin struggling to push past the exhaustion.

Pan nodded, letting his hands linger over the straps of the Pisu as he adjusted one, brushing lightly against Fox's hand in the process. Fox's eyes met his, glinting with mischief, courage, and something warmer, something child-like that had nothing to do with the coming battle. Pan's chest constricted, a tension he couldn't shake, as if that brief contact held the weight of the storm itself.

"You know," Pan murmured, voice low, almost a whisper, "we'll have to practice stealth. Hook's power... it's not just his men we need to watch for."

Fox's hand rose, resting lightly on Pan's arm, almost unconsciously, a tether amid the chaos of rain and wind. "I'll watch your back," he whispered, voice soft but deliberate, the words like a secret promise meant only for Pan.

The two moved through the wet undergrowth, boots sinking into mud-slick leaves, every step a reminder of the precarious balance between survival and peril. The storm above mirrored the coil of tension in Pan's gut—the excitement, the fear, the desire for a hand to hold, a touch to anchor him amid the approaching chaos.

Finally, they reached the encampment below, the smell of rain-soaked earth mingling with smoke from past skirmishes and the faint, acrid tang of burnt rope. The Pisu were laid down with care, the tools of their hunt positioned for easy reach. Bell's glow flickered softly nearby, wings brushing against her tiny frame as she hovered, tiny hands adjusting the younger boys' grips, her magic threading through the air like silken ribbons.

Pan's eyes followed her, memorizing every subtle motion—the tilt of her head, the flare of her wings, the faint pulse of her magic, warmer and more intimate the closer she was.

Tiger Lily's gaze cut across the camp, serious and assessing, shadowed by the dark clouds overhead. "The spot on the mountain could be compromised," she warned, crossing her arms, the muscles in her jaw taut with concern.

Pan ran a hand through his rain-soaked hair, muscles tight, fingers trembling slightly—not from cold, but from the storm of emotions whirling inside him. "You don't think I know that?" he muttered, low, almost breathless. "Magic or no, we have to trust what we can do."

Bell's small hand brushed against his shoulder, grounding him in a way no words could. He swallowed hard, aware of the heat radiating from her, the flutter of her pulse beneath his fingers, and the ache of something unspoken threading through his chest. The touch anchored him, reminded him why he fought, why he led, why he risked everything.

Voices rose in hushed arguments among the boys, tensions coiling like snakes beneath the storm. Some called for caution, others for action, and the storm overhead seemed to mirror their discord, the wind tearing at fabric and hair alike. When Bell finally spoke, her jingle carried a rare gravity, a weight both tender and unyielding.

"They aren't ready, Pan. I vote the boys stay behind," she signed, small fingers twisting the charms around her wrist, eyes shadowed with worry. The glow surrounding her pulsed faintly, each beat a tether of emotion she extended toward him.

Pan's heart tightened, a painful ache threading through his chest as he looked toward the forest beyond the camp. He knew she was right, knew that the boys' safety demanded restraint, yet the pull of wanting them all together, under his protection, burned through him like wildfire. His gaze flicked to Bell, who hovered slightly apart, wings drooping under the weight of concern, and a pang of longing dug into him—longing for her presence, for the reassurance in her hand, for the small, grounding pulse of warmth that had become his anchor in the storm.

Stepping closer, letting the rain bead across their shoulders, he murmured, voice low, roughened by both the storm and unspoken desire, "I think we need to have a little chat, old friend."

The space between them carried a heavy, intimate tension, the storm around them fading into near silence as each second stretched. The air between Pan and Bell hummed with danger, desire, and loyalty, all inextricably intertwined. The pull of the boys at his side, steady and warm, juxtaposed with the glow of Bell hovering near, magical and radiant, and Pan felt himself caught, tethered by hearts and hands he had come to trust in ways both physical and profound.

Bell moved first, a hesitant tilt forward, the faint shimmer of her wings dimming as if even the light wished to listen. Pan didn't think — he couldn't. His hand found hers, fingers cold and trembling, and in the hush that followed, their foreheads brushed. For a moment, that was enough.

Then Bell's breath caught, and her lips met his in the barest whisper of a kiss — soft, fleeting, but searing in its honesty. The world narrowed to the warmth of her mouth, the scent of rain and wild air, and the quiet ache of everything they couldn't say. When they parted, neither spoke. Only the wind dared move between them, carrying away what little remained of their restraint.

The forest swallowed them in shadows, mist curling around their boots and legs, wet leaves clinging to their clothing as if nature itself held its breath. Pan felt, for the first time that night, utterly exposed—to the world, to the battle looming below, to the ones he loved in secret, and to the storm of emotions he had long tried to suppress. Desire, fear, loyalty, responsibility—all coiled around him, taut as the lines of a bow.

He glanced toward Hook's distant figure, violin in hand, and felt the familiar sting of threat mixed with the dangerous familiarity of their history. Hook's smirk, dark and intimate, promised chaos, yet Pan's gaze drifted back to the bonds that held him together in this moment.

Bell's glow, Hook's shadow that hovered above them, —two anchors, two heartbeats, each tethered to him in ways that complicated the clarity of battle and the precision of leadership.

The rain intensified, lashing against the camp, drumming on leaves, wood, and armor, each dropping a percussion that mirrored the storm of thoughts within Pan's mind. He could hear the whisper of the Pisu straps, the scuff of Fox's boots, the soft flicker of Bell's wings cutting through the moist air. Every sound threaded into the rising tension, a symphony of preparation, danger, and intimacy.

Pan's fingers itched to touch Bell's hand, to brush a lock of wet hair from her face, yet he knew he had to remain vigilant. Every movement carried stakes beyond themselves; a single misstep could unravel plans, cost lives, or ignite Hook's wrath in ways they could not contain.

And yet, amid the storm and tension, amid the threat of battle and Hook's looming shadow, Pan allowed himself one deep breath, one moment to feel the pulse of those he trusted, the faint shimmer of Bell's magic, the grounding warmth of the boys beside him, and the weight of Neverland's fragile hope pressing on his shoulders. The ache of desire, loyalty, and responsibility all intertwined, coiling and uncoiling like the serpentine clouds above, a reminder that some battles were not only fought with swords, magic, and strategy—they were fought in hearts, in whispered promises, and in the dangerous intimacy of trust earned and shared in silence.

With that thought, Pan squared his shoulders, adjusted the Pisu across his back, and prepared to descend into the chaos below, carrying more than weapons and armor. He carried the tethered hearts of those he loved, the weight of a land at the edge of darkness, and the silent, electric promise that whatever happened, they would face it together—Pan, Bell, and the boys—bound in ways both tender and perilous, as lightning split the sky above and the storm raged on.

Chapter 27: The Meeting

The camp lay restless beneath the heavy breath of the coming storm. Fires burned low, their light flickering across tired faces and the glint of sharpened blades. Boys whispered in the dark, some praying, others laughing too loudly, the sound brittle and uncertain. Pan stood at the edge of it all, watching the shadows twist over their tents like restless spirits.

He should have felt ready—he'd planned, trained, led them here—but something inside him thrummed too loudly, too wildly. Bell's kiss still lingered on his lips, ghostlike and fragile, and it terrified him more than the battle waiting beyond the trees. Every choice he'd made, every life he'd touched, pressed against him until he could hardly breathe.

"I just need a moment," he muttered to no one in particular. A few of the boys looked up, concern flashing in their eyes, but Pan only managed a faint, reassuring smile before stepping into the trees.

The forest greeted him like an old secret—cool, damp, and alive. Each step carried him further from the warmth of the firelight, deeper into the hush between heartbeats. The mist gathered low, curling around his boots as if trying to hold him back, but he pressed on. He needed the silence. He needed to remember who he was before the blood, before the battle, before the weight of everyone's hope became too much to bear.

Pan's boots sank slightly into the damp earth, leaves clinging to his soles as he spun toward the voice that sliced through the shadows like a knife. The forest seemed to hold its breath, the wind caught in the branches, the night thick with mist and the faint, acrid tang of smoke from distant fires. And there he was—the man who haunted his nightmares, the shadow that lingered at the edge of every plan, every heartbeat, every whispered dream.

Hook stepped from the darkened trees, his movements deliberate, calm. Moonlight traced the hard edges of his face—the scars, the sharpness that age had honed rather than softened. His coat was damp, his hair streaked with gray, his eyes the same deep, cutting blue Pan remembered from long ago. For a moment, they only stared at each other—teacher and student, reflection and shadow.

"What are you doing here?" Pan's voice came out rougher than he intended. "Shouldn't you be hiding behind your men, waiting for dawn?"

Hook's mouth twitched, not quite a smile. "Still quick with your tongue. I taught you that too."

Pan bristled, the words striking too close to memory. "You didn't teach me everything."

"No," Hook said quietly. "Not everything. You stopped listening before I could." He took another step forward, slow and unthreatening, but every motion was charged with authority. "You shouldn't be out here alone, Peter. You're leading boys into a war you don't understand."

Pan's grip tightened on his weapon. "And whose fault is that? You left before you could finish the lesson."

Hook's jaw flexed. "Because you thought you were ready. Because you *wanted* to be me." His voice hardened—steel wrapped in grief. "You don't know what that means."

Pan laughed under his breath, short and bitter. "No? I learned it from watching you burn everything you cared about."

That landed like a blow. Hook didn't answer at first. When he finally spoke, his voice was low, almost hoarse. "I made mistakes. I paid for them. But you—" His tone sharpened. "You still have a chance to be better."

"Better?" Pan echoed. "Better than you? Better than the man who taught me how to fight, how to lead, how to *survive*?" His eyes flashed, anger breaking through his restraint. "Every boy in that camp believes in me because you showed me how to make them believe. Don't pretend you didn't make me what I am."

Hook's expression flickered—something like pride, quickly buried beneath sorrow. "I know exactly what I made you. That's why I'm here."

Silence hung between them, heavy as the mist. The forest felt smaller, closing in around their words.

"Come with me," Hook said at last, voice gentler now. "To the Lagoon. We can end this before it begins. Your boys don't have to die. None of them do."

Pan's eyes narrowed. "And what—walk away from everything we've fought for? Hand you Neverland on a silver plate?"

Hook's tone sharpened. "You think this is about Neverland? About territory? Peter, look at yourself. You're fighting a war you don't even understand because you can't let go of your pride."

Pan's jaw clenched. "That's rich, coming from you."

Hook's eyes flared. "I *led* men into battles that never should have been fought. I buried good soldiers—friends—because I couldn't stop myself. Don't make the same mistake."

For a moment, the storm seemed to pause around them. Pan's breath came hard, his heart a drumbeat against his ribs. The way Hook spoke—like a commander trying to save a soldier, like a father pleading with a son—unraveled something deep in him.

"You always talk like you care," Pan said, voice cracking despite himself. "But you're the reason I learned to fight in the first place."

Hook's reply came soft, worn by years of regret. "I didn't teach you to fight. I taught you to survive. I just never imagined you'd have to use it against me."

The words hit harder than any weapon could.

Pan swallowed, throat tight. "You should go, Hook. Before I make good on every reason they call you my enemy."

Hook looked at him for a long moment—really looked at him. Then, almost imperceptibly, he nodded. "You're ready," he said quietly. "But that's what frightens me most."

He turned to leave, his voice carrying faintly through the thickening rain. "When dawn comes, Peter, I'll fight you if I must. But know this—everything you are, everything you've become... part of that will always be mine."

Pan stood there long after he disappeared into the mist, the sound of rain swallowing the forest whole. His fingers trembled around his weapon, heart pounding with anger, grief, and something that felt like mourning.

For the man who had once been his teacher.
 For the father he never truly had.
 And for the boy he no longer was.

Chapter 28: Reluction

The forest seemed quieter on the walk back, but Pan's mind roared. Every step felt heavier, every crackle of leaves beneath his boots a reminder of Hook's voice, his words, his presence. He clenched and unclenched his fists, trying to force himself into the routine of a leader—the calm, steady Peter Pan the boys expected.

By the time he reached the camp, the fires had dimmed further, shadows pooling in the corners of the tents. A few boys stirred, whispering, stretching, checking weapons. Pan swallowed hard, forcing his shoulders down, forcing his jaw to relax, forcing his pulse to slow.

"Peter?" A boy's voice called softly. Slight, careful. Pan shook his head and gave a faint, tight smile. "All good," he said, voice steady, too steady. He turned away before the boy could press further, striding toward the center of camp as if nothing had happened.

But nothing had *happened*, had it? His chest ached, tight and unyielding, and the words Hook had left lingering in the mist scraped against the inside of his skull. *"You're ready. But that's what frightens me most."*

Pan ground his teeth, scanning the camp. Boys were checking blades, stacking firewood, whispering in groups—but all he could see were the memories: Hook's eyes, the quiet sorrow behind the anger, the faint nod when he'd said, *"You're ready."* The lessons, the warnings, the grief.

He forced himself to speak when a boy tripped nearby. "Watch your step." The words came out clipped, sharper than intended. The boy looked up at him, startled, and Pan caught the flash of fear, the silent question in the boy's eyes: *What's wrong with him?*

Pan turned quickly, moving toward the fire, letting the heat lick at his damp coat. He tried to ground himself, tried to remind himself he was Peter Pan—the fearless, untouchable leader of the Lost Boys. Yet every corner of his mind was crowded with Hook's warnings, his eyes, the ache of a mentorship lost and now impossible.

He paced, restless. The menacing calm that Hook carried was infectious, leaving Pan off balance. *Control yourself,* he thought, gripping his own forearm. But restraint felt brittle, like ice about to snap.

A hand on his shoulder made him start. He spun, but it was only Nibs, eyes wide with concern. "You're quiet tonight, Peter. You're... different."

Pan forced a laugh, low and humorless. "Just thinking. Nothing more." He stepped back, brushing off the hand, desperate to reclaim the authority he knew he had to project. But even as he barked out instructions to the boys—check weapons, patrol the perimeter, keep the fire going—his voice trembled just enough to betray him. Just enough for anyone watching closely to see that something had unsettled him deeply.

When the boys finally settled, Pan lingered at the edge of the firelight, staring into the flickering flames as if trying to burn away Hook's shadow. His jaw ached from holding back words, from swallowing anger, grief, and... something he wasn't ready to name. The forest outside whispered and shifted, echoing the storm still raging inside him.

He hated the vulnerability, the ache, the way Hook's words clung to him like smoke. And yet—he couldn't shake them. He was a boy trained to lead, trained to fight, trained to survive. But the man who had once been his teacher had reminded him of what he feared most: that growing up meant carrying weight he couldn't yet put down.

Pan clenched his fists again, hard, letting the nails dig into his palms. He would hide it from the boys. He had to. But even as he forced himself to smile at the next question, to answer every inquiry with calm authority, deep down he knew: nothing in the camp, nothing in Neverland, would ever feel the same.

Hook's presence lingered in the night, a ghost pressing on the boy he had made, and the Lost Boys would never see the storm behind the eyes of their leader.

Chapter 29: Hallucinations

The first skirmish came sooner than expected.
The Lost Boys had barely moved from the edge
of camp when shadows slithered through the
trees, figures too fast and silent to be counted
easily. Pan's orders were crisp, but his mind was
elsewhere—Hook's voice echoing in his head,
the weight of every lesson and every warning
pressing against him like iron.

"Hold the line!" he shouted, but even as he said
it, he felt the old, reckless fire flare in his chest.
The instinct to rush, to confront, to *do everything
himself*—the same instinct Hook had scolded
him for years ago—overrode careful strategy.

He spun toward a shadow moving too close to
Nibs, launching himself into the fight with a
ferocity that shocked even the older boys. A
single misstep, a blade swung too wide, and he
could have taken out one of his own. His pulse
roared in his ears, adrenaline drowning out logic.

"Peter—wait!" the soft jingle echoing from the edge of the camp.

Bell.

He froze mid-strike, the forest spinning around him as his grip faltered. She was there, eyes wide, her expression a mixture of concern and incredulity. "Peter, what are you doing? You've been... acting off all night! What happened?"

Pan lowered his weapon, breathing hard. For a moment he considered brushing her off, pretending nothing had changed. But the weight in his chest—the lingering sting of Hook's words—was too heavy to keep buried. "I... I saw Hook," he admitted, voice low. "I spoke with him."

Bell's eyes narrowed, the sharp edge of anger flashing through her usual calm. "*You what?*"

"He said... he said I'm ready," Pan continued, struggling to maintain the authority in his voice he knew the boys needed. "He offered to end the fighting, let the Lost Boys go… if I came with him."

Bell stepped closer, hands angrily waving around with her words, rain dripping from her hair. Her eyes burned with disbelief and frustration. "You *should have signaled the alarm!* We could've ended this before it even started! This was reckless, Peter. You could have—" She cut herself off, shaking her head. "You *didn't even think about the boys.*"

Pan's jaw tightened. "I know. I know I didn't. But… he's not just an enemy, Bell. He's… he's everything I've ever learned from, everything I've ever tried to surpass. I—" His voice faltered. "I couldn't ignore him. I can't ignore him."

Bell's expression softened for a moment, but her anger didn't waver. "You need to stop acting like this is a game. Leadership isn't about proving yourself to ghosts from your past, Peter. It's about keeping these boys alive. About making smart choices!"

Pan's fists clenched, rain soaking his coat. "You don't understand—he's part of why I *am* who I am. I can't just... throw that away!"

"And what if throwing that away is exactly what saves lives?" Bell shot back, movements sharp but trembling slightly from the weight of fear. "We could've ended this now, before any blood is spilled! Before anyone else gets hurt!"

Pan stared at her, chest tightening, the storm inside him raging. Every instinct screamed to prove himself, to act, to take the fight to Hook, to show he could handle everything on his own. Yet Bell's words struck at the other part—the part of him that wanted to protect the boys, that wanted to be more than the impulsive, reckless shadow Hook had trained him to be.

"I... I don't know what's right anymore," he admitted, voice low, almost a whisper. His eyes flicked to the misted tree line, imagining Hook watching, waiting, measuring. "I just... I can't stop thinking about him."

Bell placed a hand gently on his arm, grounding him. "Peter... listen to me. You're not fighting him alone. Not anymore. You have us. You have me. You don't have to carry everything from your past into the battle."

For a moment, Pan closed his eyes, letting her words settle against the storm in his chest. The adrenaline slowed, the recklessness dimmed—but only slightly. The pull of Hook's shadow lingered, a weight he knew he'd have to confront, even as the forest outside braced for the first clash.

Pan opened his eyes, grim determination settling over him. "You're right," he said, voice firmer. "But I... I won't fail. Not the boys. Not you. Not him."

Bell nodded, but her expression remained wary. "Then lead wisely. And Peter..." Her gaze hardened, a quiet warning. "Next time, *don't let your past decide our future.*"

Pan nodded, swallowing hard, letting the firelight flicker across his tense features. He had survived the encounter with Hook—but the battle with himself was far from over.

Chapter 30: Calm Before the Storm

The forest hung in an uneasy silence, the calm before the storm. Rain dripped steadily from the canopy, pattering softly against leaves and mud, masking the distant rustle of movement. The Lost Boys crouched in scattered groups, weapons at the ready, eyes darting through the gloom, alert to the slightest shift in shadow. Fires burned low, casting long, wavering lines across the damp ground, but the usual warmth they brought seemed muted under the weight of expectation.

Pan sat alone atop a fallen tree, shoulders tense, fists clenched, eyes scanning the treeline as if it could tell him what Hook planned next. His breathing was measured, but only barely; every instinct throbbed with urgency, every nerve sang with the desire to strike before the enemy could. He could feel the storm of adrenaline coiling in his chest, tightening with each heartbeat.

"Peter..." Bell's voice broke the quiet, soft but firm. She hovered nearby, wings folded close, trying to anchor him with her presence. "You need to stay calm. The boys are ready. You're ready. Take a breath. Focus."

Pan's jaw tightened. He wanted to obey, wanted to ground himself, wanted to let strategy guide him.

But every lesson Hook had ever taught, every ghost of a memory, pushed him toward recklessness. "I can't calm down, Bell," he muttered, voice low and harsh. "He's here. He's out there, and I can *feel* him watching, waiting…"

Bell stepped closer, hand brushing against his arm. "Then *don't* go looking for him alone. Trust the boys. Trust me. We'll—"

A deep, sonorous horn ripped through the forest before she could finish, vibrating through the trees and mud, shaking the air around them. Pan's head snapped toward the sound, eyes wide and alight with immediate, raw urgency. The horn sounded again, longer, echoing, commanding, and it carried the unmistakable weight of Hook's ship—right on the edge of the bay, closer than anyone had expected.

Pan leapt to his feet, the momentum of his body matching the thundering of his heartbeat. "Get ready! Everyone, *now*! Weapons, positions, shields!" he shouted, voice slicing through the mist like a blade.

Bell's wings flared as she rose to match him, hands outstretched, trying to meet his intensity with reason. "Peter, wait! Don't let the horn push you into—"

But he was already moving, dashing between the trees, shouting orders, snapping the boys into formation, his energy spilling over like a storm unbound. Every word, every gesture, every movement was charged with desperation. Bell tried to catch his gaze, to ground him, but he barely noticed. The forest blurred around him, his focus zeroed entirely on the threat she could only just sense: Hook, imminent and waiting, his shadow stretching across the trees before he had even arrived.

"Left flank, Nibs! Cover the ridge!" Pan barked, spinning toward another group of boys. "Don't let them break through! Tootles! Hold the fire!"

Bell followed, wings beating fast, trying to keep pace and keep him from throwing himself into the very danger she feared. "Peter! Listen to me!" she called, voice cutting through the chaos. "Control your fury! Control your *focus*! You're not invincible!"

But her words only reached half of his mind. Pan was already scanning the forest, already moving toward the movement he could sense beyond the trees—the glint of cutlass hilts, the flash of metal, the faint reflection of Hook's coat in the mist. His hands shook, adrenaline and anticipation colliding, pulling him forward, and Bell realized she was losing him in the very chaos she had tried to prevent.

He barked another order, signaling the boys to hold their positions, but the tension in his shoulders betrayed his lack of control. The storm inside him was spilling outward, pushing him toward the enemy, toward the man he had trained to surpass, toward Hook himself.

Bell's wings beat faster, carrying her ahead, trying to intercept him before he did something irrevocable. "Peter, *stop!*" she cried, but he had already vanished into the edge of the forest, leaving only the echo of his voice and the promise of impending battle behind.

The horn sounded again, a low, resonant call that seemed to shake the very ground beneath their boots. The Lost Boys stiffened in their positions, ready for the attack, but Pan's shadow was gone among the trees, a streak of green and reckless energy racing toward Hook, untethered, unstoppable, and unaware that Bell was now his only barrier against the storm he was about to unleash.

The forest held its breath.

Chapter 31: The Weight of Recklessness

Pan tore through the misted forest, every instinct screaming forward, his boots sliding through mud, branches snagging his coat. The Lost Boys were positioned behind him, firing arrows and swinging slingshots, but his eyes never left Hook. He could see the faint glimmer of the captain's coat ahead, the measured movement of his soldiers, and all Pan could think was *I can do this. I can end this. I have to.*

"Hold the line! Don't let them flank!" Pan barked over his shoulder, but even as the words left his lips, he knew he wasn't giving orders so much as issuing excuses for his own recklessness.

A volley of arrows streaked past, one grazing Nibs' shoulder. Pan cursed under his breath. *If only I were faster... closer...* He swung his dagger, slicing through the mist, his movements precise, but his focus was entirely on Hook. Every instinct Hook had ever instilled in him—the fire, the speed, the audacity—pushed him forward, overriding any sense of caution.

"Peter! Stop!" Bell's voice echoed through the chaos. She flitted between the boys, guiding arrows, repositioning fighters, but always keeping her eyes on him. "You're going to get yourself killed! Control yourself!"

"I've got this!" he shouted back, voice strained, heart hammering. "I *can* do this!"

Bell caught up to him just as he ducked under a sweeping cut from one of Hook's lieutenants. She grabbed his arm, yanking him back just enough to avoid the strike. "No! This isn't about proving yourself! Not today!"

Pan jerked away, frustration and adrenaline coiling into a dangerous tension. "He's right there! I can end this!" His voice cracked, almost a growl. "I have to!"

"You're being reckless!" Bell snapped, planting herself firmly between him and the enemy, wings flared and rain slicking her hair to her face. "Do you *want* the boys to die while you play the hero?"

Pan's gaze flicked to the Lost Boys. Some were wounded, some were straining to hold their positions against the overwhelming numbers, and his chest twisted. Every instinct screamed to surge forward, to carry the fight to Hook himself, to prove he was worthy of everything Hook had ever taught him… and more.

He lunged again. Bell caught him, spinning him aside, and for a heartbeat they collided in the mud and rain, his anger crashing against her steady resistance. "Peter, *listen to me*! You're not invincible! You're not a one-man army!"

Pan's fingers flexed, nails digging into the mud beneath him. "I... I can't just wait!" he hissed. "I *have* to act now, before they..." He couldn't finish the thought. Every ounce of caution, every strategic plan, had been drowned out by the fire Hook had lit inside him years ago.

A shadow flickered ahead. Hook himself stepped into the clearing, soldiers fanning out behind him, weapons raised, eyes gleaming with calculated calm. Pan's stomach tightened, but the fire in his chest flared brighter than fear. He surged forward again, belligerent, impulsive, unstoppable.

"Peter!" Bell shouted, wings beating furiously. "Stop!"

But he was past her. She ran after him, dodging through soldiers, throwing herself between him and the strikes that came too close. She reached him just as he brought his dagger down toward Hook, who raised a hand to parry—and then stepped back, calmly, almost teasingly.

"You're predictable, Peter," Hook said, voice low and cutting, eyes flashing with cold amusement. "Always rushing, always burning your own path, always thinking you can carry the weight of everything."

Pan skidded to a halt, chest heaving, but his hands still shook with tension. Hook's soldiers fanned out around him, and the Lost Boys were holding the line further back, firing and dodging, but unable to prevent Hook from slipping further into the trees.

Bell planted herself firmly between Pan and Hook, arms outstretched, wings beating through the storm. "I *will not* let you do this alone! I *will not* let you throw yourself away!" she yelled. Her voice carried over the chaos, a lifeline, a tether pulling him back from the edge of his impulsive fury.

Pan froze, eyes blazing, chest tight. He wanted to strike, to prove himself, to end Hook once and for all—but Bell's presence anchored him, if only barely. Her gaze met his, firm and unwavering, and he felt the fragile weight of responsibility, of leadership, of the boys behind him, pressing down with impossible force.

Hook's hand moved to his holster, fingers brushing the gun, eyes flicking between Pan and Bell. Calm. Calculated. Patient. Every instinct in Pan screamed to leap forward, to strike before Hook could act.

Bell sensed it too, wings flaring, body tensed in a protective stance. "Peter, *now is not the time!* Stand down!"

But the seconds stretched into eternity. Hook's finger tightened on the trigger. The forest seemed to hold its breath. The rain pelted down, the Lost

Boys were shouting, the mist swirled around their feet, and Pan felt the full weight of his impulsive choices, the dangerous fire Hook had stoked in him for years.

And then—

Bang.

The gunshot ripped through the forest, echoing, deafening, slicing through the storm. Bell's wings flared as she shielded Pan instinctively, her voice a sharp cry against the roar of the rain.

Pan's chest slammed into his lungs, adrenaline spiking, ears ringing. The world contracted to a single moment: Hook's gun, Bell between them, the Lost Boys holding their precarious line, and the knowledge that everything he had learned, everything Hook had taught him, everything he had tried to control… had erupted into chaos, and the consequences were about to hit them all.

Chapter 32: Rain and Ruin

The crack of the gunshot still reverberated in Pan's ears, sharp and final. The world seemed to tilt as Bell collapsed to the forest floor, wings flaring in a desperate, futile attempt to stay upright. Her chest sagged against the rain-soaked mud, a crimson bloom spreading across her coat, and the color drained from Pan's vision in an instant.

"No… no, no, no!" Pan's voice tore through the chaos, raw and jagged. He skidded to her side, mud splattering across his boots, hands trembling as he pressed against the wound. "Bell! Stay with me! Don't… don't you dare leave me!"

The Lost Boys froze, mid-combat, the shouts and clashes of the skirmish fading as the full horror of what had happened struck them. Tootles and Nibs scrambled forward, slipping in the mud, trying to assist, but Pan waved them off fiercely. "No! Back! Help the others hold the line!"

Bell's hand twitched slightly under his grip. Her eyes opened, pain and shock clouding their usual brilliance. "Peter…" she rasped, voice weak, voice cutting straight to his chest. "You… you have to… lead… the boys…"

Pan shook his head violently, pressing his hands harder to her wound, panic surging like wildfire.

"No! I'm not leaving you! You're not dying on me, Bell, you hear me? *You're not!*"

Her lips quivered faintly in the ghost of a smile. "Go... after Hook... Peter... you..."

Pan's chest constricted, heart hammering, rage and guilt and fear colliding in a storm so violent it left him nearly paralyzed. *After Hook... or save her...* His body trembled. Every instinct screamed to surge forward, to chase down the man who had haunted him, to strike back for all the lessons, all the torment, all the reckless fire Hook had instilled in him.

But Bell's gaze, weak but steady, anchored him. Her hand twitched against his arm as if pulling him back from the edge. "Peter... choose... them... choose..."

The forest blurred around him—the Lost Boys still fighting, Hook's forces advancing, the rain blurring visibility—but Pan made a decision that nearly broke him. He could chase Hook later. He could strike him down another day. But Bell... Bell was here, bleeding, depending on him. And these boys... these boys were *all he had.*

"I... I'm not leaving you," Pan whispered, voice trembling with both resolve and raw panic. He scooped Bell up into his arms, her body limp and light against his chest, wings drooping uselessly against his shoulder. "I've got you. I've got you,

Bell. We're going back. Stay with me. Please... just stay with me."

The Lost Boys fell into a tense retreat, dragging the wounded behind Pan and keeping Hook's forces at a cautious distance. Rain stung Pan's eyes as he stumbled through the mud, heart hammering, every muscle taut with fear and urgency. "Keep moving! Don't stop! We're going back! We're alive and we're going back!" he yelled, voice raw, cracking under the strain of command and terror.

Every shadow made him flinch. Every distant shout of Hook's soldiers made him tense, nearly pivoting toward the danger, fighting against the instinct to turn and charge. But Bell's weight in his arms, her faint, shallow breaths, kept him tethered. He stumbled, slipped, nearly fell, but tightened his grip on her, murmuring, "I've got you... I've got you... just hold on..."

The forest felt endless, the mist thick, obscuring the path, but Pan's focus narrowed to the warmth of her form, the rhythm of her breathing, the fragile life he was carrying. Every step he took was frantic, desperate, and raw, a mixture of fear and guilt and overwhelming love.

The boys fell in behind him, scrambling to keep up, mud-slicked and exhausted, but Pan barely noticed. His world had contracted to two things: Bell, and getting her back to the safety of the camp. Hook's horn sounded faintly in the distance, a reminder that the battle was far from over, but Pan could not risk it—not now.

Finally, through a tangle of roots and fallen branches, they reached a small clearing near the camp. Pan lowered Bell gently onto a mossy patch, brushing rain-soaked hair from her face. Her breathing was shallow, uneven, but she was alive. He knelt beside her, hands pressed against her wound, murmuring frantic reassurances, "You're okay... you're going to be okay... don't you leave me, Bell... don't you *dare*..."

The Lost Boys formed a protective circle around them, faces pale and frightened, weapons ready, but Pan barely saw them. His eyes never left Bell. He was trembling violently now, sweat and rain mingling on his brow, voice raw from shouting. "You're not going anywhere. I promise. I won't let anything happen to you. Not Hook... not anyone. Stay with me..."

Somewhere in the distance, Hook's horn sounded again, lower this time, taunting. The forest trembled with the promise of more battle. But for this moment, Pan could only focus on the fragile weight in his arms, on Bell's shallow breaths, on the crushing guilt and panic gnawing at him for having let his impulsiveness put her in danger.

He rocked her gently, whispering to her through the pounding rain and the tremors of his own fear.

"You're going to make it, Bell… I won't let you die…
I won't… I swear…"

And though the battle raged around them, Pan
stayed there, frantic and trembling, holding the one
person who had always kept him grounded,
knowing he had finally chosen responsibility over
recklessness—for now.

Chapter 33: Cocoon of Gold

Pan stumbled through the forest, Bell cradled in his arms, until he reached the small grove where the younger Lost Boys had stayed back, hidden from the full brunt of Hook's assault.

The soft glow of the firelight illuminated the worried faces of the boys, and the air carried a mixture of smoke, rain, and the faint scent of herbs from the small group of Le Clan de L'Aura Radieuse who had accompanied them. Among them, Tiger Lily's presence stood out, calm but sharp-eyed, her expression unreadable beneath the hood of her cloak.

"Here," Pan gasped, lowering Bell carefully onto the mossy floor, mud and rain slicking her damp hair. Her wings fluttered weakly, the glittering luminescence fading like a dying star. Panic knotted his chest, making his hands shake as he pressed them against her side in a futile attempt to stop the tremor in his own body.

The healers from the clan immediately knelt around her, murmuring softly, their voices rising and falling in a rhythm that seemed to pulse with the heartbeat of the forest itself. Hands traced intricate patterns in the air, weaving delicate sigils that shimmered faintly against the mist, calling on the threads of magic that lingered in the soil and rain-soaked leaves.

Small sparks of light flickered along their fingertips, like fireflies caught in a slow, deliberate dance, and crushed herbs were sprinkled carefully over Bell's chest and wings, releasing fragrant puffs that mingled with the earthy scent of the forest.

Pan's gaze never left her face, every flicker of movement, every shallow breath, sending waves of tension through him. The magic began to intensify, coalescing around Bell in a soft, luminescent glow that painted the rain in shades of emerald. It swirled over her form like living silk, curling along her wings and tracing the lines of her delicate body, illuminating her in a surreal, otherworldly light.

The green shimmer deepened and pulsed, resonating with the quiet hum of the healers' chants, before slowly shifting, melting into threads of pure gold that rippled across her chest and limbs. The glow wrapped around her like a cocoon, warm and vibrant, radiating an almost tangible energy that made the mist shimmer and the rain seem to slow, as if the forest itself had bent its attention to her survival. Tiny motes of golden light floated upward, suspended in the humid air, drifting like sparks from a gentle flame before being absorbed back into the cocoon around her.

Pan's hands trembled despite the magic, hovering near her but never touching, afraid to disrupt the delicate weave. He could feel the power resonating, almost vibrating through him, and for a brief, suspended moment, the storm of guilt and fear receded, replaced by awe at the raw, living energy of the healers' work.

Yet even as the golden glow intensified, Pan knew that it was fragile—that one wrong movement, one hesitation, one mistake, and everything could unravel. And so he stayed, tense, trembling, and utterly vigilant, watching, willing, praying for the magic to hold.

"She's strong," one of the healers whispered to him, voice calm but firm. "Strong enough to hold on. But this is beyond simple mending. You must stay close."

Pan nodded, hands trembling, as he shifted slightly to keep Bell warm against his chest. The boys clustered around, fear and uncertainty etched into their faces. Tootles fiddled nervously with his sling, Nibs bit down on his lip, and even the younger ones pressed close but stayed silent, as though their quiet fear might somehow help.

Tiger Lily finally stepped forward, her eyes locking on Pan's face, sharp and unflinching. "Peter," she said softly, but with the authority that cut through the chaos, "what happened?"

Pan swallowed, his throat tight, heart hammering in a way that matched the pounding of the storm outside. He couldn't hide it. Not from her. Not now. He followed her to the edge of the small clearing, keeping Bell within his line of sight, and finally let himself collapse into a low, ragged breath.

"It… it was my fault," he admitted, voice shaking. "I was reckless. I… I went after him. I went after Hook, and I didn't—" His voice broke, the weight of guilt pressing on him like stones. "I didn't protect her. I… I put Bell in danger. My actions—everything I did—it's what caused this."

Tiger Lily's expression softened slightly, but her eyes remained steady, piercing. "You made a choice," she said, tone even, almost a teacher's calm scolding. "A dangerous one. And now you are facing the consequences. That is the truth you must carry, Peter."

Pan's hands clenched into fists, trembling at his sides. "I should have stayed back," he whispered, voice nearly lost in the rain drumming overhead. "I should have listened… but I couldn't. I couldn't just let him… I thought I could—" His teeth gritted. "I thought I could stop him on my own, and now she's… she's—"

"She is not gone," Tiger Lily interrupted, placing a hand on his shoulder, grounding him. "And she *will* survive if you focus, if you *hold yourself together*. The panic will not help her. Only your calm, your presence, your… restraint, can give her a chance to heal."

Pan swallowed hard, eyes flicking back to Bell's fading wings. He wanted to scream, to cry, to charge back into the forest after Hook and unleash every ounce of fire he had, but Tiger Lily's calm, steady presence anchored him. For now, he will stay. For now, he would let the healers do their work. For now, he would *be responsible*.

He sank to the floor beside Bell, hands pressed gently over hers as if that could transfer strength, murmuring softly to her, "Stay with me... stay with me, Bell. You have to... you have to stay."

Tiger Lily watched him for a moment longer, then stepped back, letting Pan sit with the fairy he had nearly lost, her wings slowly flickering faintly with the magic of the clan. The Lost Boys hovered close, glances flitting between Pan and Bell, afraid to move, afraid to speak, but drawn to the quiet desperation of their leader.

And in that fragile silence, heavy with rain, guilt, and the weight of his impulsiveness, Pan realized something he had long refused to face: strength was not just speed, or fire, or fury—it was restraint. It was patience. It was knowing when to fight, and when to stay, and when to protect those who could not protect themselves.

Chapter 34: The Measure of a Leader

Hours passed with a slow, almost unbearable weight, the forest settling into a tense lull around the small clearing. The rain had eased to a steady drizzle, but the mist lingered, curling around the mossy floor and clinging to Pan's mud-slick boots. The healers never left Bell's side, kneeling in a tight circle, murmuring incantations, their hands tracing patterns in the air as the golden-emerald glow pulsed gently over her fragile form. Pan remained beside her, fingers brushing lightly over her trembling wings, pressing a damp cloth to her forehead, whispering her name over and over. Every shallow breath she drew sent spikes of both relief and terror through him.

The Lost Boys moved cautiously around them, regrouping, tending to minor scrapes and mud-streaked clothing, eyes darting constantly toward Hook's distant forces. Pan's gaze rarely left Bell. He adjusted her wings, tightened her coat around her small frame, and murmured low assurances, though his voice shook despite his attempts at steadiness. He refused to leave her, refused to step back, even as exhaustion began to claw at his muscles and his mind.

And all the while, the storm inside him simmered—guilt coiled tight around his ribs, anger toward himself for letting his impulsiveness put her in danger, and the relentless itch to return to the fight, to go after Hook, to reclaim the control he had so recklessly surrendered. The golden glow around Bell shimmered and shifted, ebbing and pulsing with the delicate thread of life she clung to, and every flicker made Pan's chest tighten. *If I'd just waited… if I'd just listened…*

Tiger Lily approached silently, her presence measured and commanding, pulling him a few paces away. The air between them was heavy with rain, mist, and the faint hum of residual magic from the healers' work. "Peter," she said, voice low but sharp enough to cut through his spiraling thoughts, "you need to understand the consequences of your actions. Look at her."

Pan followed her gaze back to Bell, her wings dim but still shimmering faintly in the golden-emerald glow, and his stomach tightened further. His hands clenched into fists, trembling. "I… I thought I could—" he started, voice rough, but Tiger Lily's hand on his shoulder stopped him mid-sentence.

"You thought recklessness could solve this?" she asked, eyes piercing. "You risked *her life*, Peter. You risked the boys. And for what? A chance at vengeance? A chance to prove something to yourself?"

"I… I just wanted to stop him…" Pan muttered, eyes darting toward the edge of the forest, toward the direction where Hook had disappeared. "I can't just… I have to—"

Tiger Lily shook her head slowly. "That is precisely why you *cannot* act alone. That is precisely why leadership is not about bravado or speed. You act without thinking, and those you care about pay the price. You must control yourself, Peter. Not for Hook. Not for the battle. But for them."

The words struck him harder than any blow. Pan looked back at Bell, the subtle rise and fall of her chest, the faint glow of life persisting despite his reckless choices, and a wave of guilt crashed over him. He had survived countless fights, faced impossible odds, and yet here, his inability to restrain himself had brought her to the brink.

"I… I know," he whispered, voice breaking. "I… I can't let this happen again. I… I promise I'll—"

Tiger Lily's grip tightened on his shoulder. "No promises. You *show* it. Actions, Peter. That is the measure of a leader. Your recklessness nearly cost everything. Do you understand that?"

Pan swallowed, chest tight, eyes brimming with a mixture of shame, fear, and the restless energy still thrumming beneath the surface. He wanted to leave, to chase Hook, to feel the adrenaline of the fight, but the golden glow around Bell reminded him, painfully, of what was truly important.

"Yes," he said finally, voice low, trembling. "I understand. I... I have to be better. I *will* be better."

Tiger Lily nodded once, sharply, and stepped back, letting him return to Bell's side. The healers murmured on, hands tracing the delicate threads of magic over her wings and chest, the golden-emerald light pulsing steadily, weaving life back into her fragile form. Pan settled beside her once more, hands hovering near her trembling form, every sense alert, heart hammering, mind still torn between the urge to act and the desperate need to remain calm.

And in that fragile, tense stillness, the forest around them seemed to pause, the rain dripping slowly, the Lost Boys quietly tending each other, and Pan realized the battle had not only been against Hook—it had been against himself. And for now, at least, he had chosen restraint.

Chapter 35: Two Paths, One Promise

The war tent smelled of damp canvas, crushed herbs, and the low, lingering tang of the healers' light—gold-and-emerald motes drifting like stray embers through the entrance each time someone came or went.

A single lantern swung from the central pole, throwing jittering shadows across the rough map pinned to the table: coastlines inked in charcoal, the jagged tooth of the mountains rising like a wall, Mermaid Lagoon glossed in blue, the thinned tree-lines and marshes traced in a dozen shaky hand-drawn marks.

Tiger Lily stood with her fingers pressed to the edge of the map, jaw tight, eyes like flint in the lamplight. Pan hovered on the other side of the table, coat still streaked with mud, hair plastered to his forehead by rain, anger and exhaustion fighting just beneath the surface of his features. Between them, pensed charcoal crumbled and scattered as both spoke over the map, the tent thick with the pressure of planning—and with the unspoken weight of what had already been lost.

"We move left of the mountains," Tiger Lily said, voice low and steady, tapping the charcoal line with a callused finger. "We cut through the pine ridge there, circling down behind Hook's right flank. He expects a frontal pressure near the lagoon. He will not be ready for a silent strike from the west. The fox paths are narrow enough for ambushes; we can force them into kill zones."

Pan slammed a hand flat onto the table, making the lantern sway. "No. We go *over* the mountains," he spat, chest heaving. "Hook will never expect a force to cross those scree slopes in this weather. We use the high ground—stalk them from above. We push them down into the lagoon, split their attention. If we control the ridgeline we control sightlines, and once they're pinned, the boys can move in."

Tiger Lily's eyes didn't soften. "You think the boys can climb those slopes in this storm? The injured, the younger ones—"

"They don't go over the mountains!" Pan barked. "Not the kids. Not Bell. I said *we* use the mountains to our advantage. The climb is hard, but it's an advantage worth taking. Surprise means the quickest end."

A silence fell heavy enough to listen to. Outside, the forest murmured and the faint, steady glow from the healers' circle drifted through the tent flap like a heartbeat. Pan's jaw clenched; he could feel the old ember of recklessness trying to throttle the cautious part of him he'd promised to listen to. Tiger Lily watched him like a teacher watching a student push past a boundary. Neither of them wanted to lose more to pride.

"You want glory," she said bluntly, not cruelly, "and he'll give you an opportunity to throw it away. I want a plan that keeps our people alive."

Pan's fingers drummed the map. "I want him *gone*," he whispered. Then louder: "But not if it gets Bell killed. Not if it gets the boys killed. We can use the mountains *and* flank left—if we coordinate."

Her answer was a quiet scoff. "That spreads us thin. Hook will slice a pie out of us."

"Maybe." Pan met her eyes, raw. "Maybe he will. But if he does, at least the children and the injured will be safe. If we put the best archers up in the crags, they cover retreat and ambush; the rest of us—Clan, boys, we strike the left and draw his forces out. The mountain archers pick them off. We can bait him."

Tiger Lily did not give ground easily. "You would split our force in half during the first counterattack?"

"We split the exposure," Pan countered. "We make his risk greater than ours. We keep the crits—kids and healers—out of the open while we force him into chokepoints."

For several long minutes they circled the same words, the same contours of ink on the map. Tiger

Lily pushed and prodded over routes, estimated march-times, the risk of scree and avalanche, the number of men Hook could bring to bear. Pan argued sightlines, surprise, and the advantage of unpredictable verticality. Each time Tiger Lily countered with caution, Pan matched with the passionate almost-desperation of a leader who had nearly lost the person he loved. Between strategy and sentiment the tent vibrated with tension.

Then the flap rustled and three of the boys who'd been in the last assault slipped in, rain-hushed and mud-smeared. Tootles with his sleeve torn, Nibs leaning on a splint, and Curly, eyes wide and steady though his face was streaked with grime. They hesitated at the threshold, then straightened and stepped inside, glancing first at Bell's temporary shelter in the grove beyond and then to the two arguing figures.

"We heard you," Tootles said simply, voice rough. "We were out there. We saw them move. We... We tried to hold it. We don't want to be left behind." He shook his head, earnest. "But we know both of you are right."

Pan and Tiger Lily both looked at them like a slow sunrise—awareness dawning. Tootles' gaze flicked to the map and then to Tiger Lily. "If we go only left, Hook will loop round and drown the kids in the lagoon if he splits forces." Then to Pan: "If we go only over the mountain, the boys with the slings won't hold long enough to stop the scouts."

Nibs cut in, voice blunt as a thrown rock. "We took a beating last time because we tried to hold too big a line. Spread thin is bad—unless one side is a trap. If we put the kids and strongest archers up high, they can rain ruin on anyone who comes near the mountain paths. They'll be safe in the ridgeline cover."

Curly nodded. "Clan archers are better than us with bows. Put the youngest with them; they'll keep watch and cover. Hide them in the limestone—caves and overhangs. The mountain holds many shadows. The rest of us—Clan and Lost Boys—sweep left of Mermaid Lagoon and force Hook into a funnel."

The three boys spoke like boys who had seen fire and wanted no more of it, and their simple, practical solution hit a note both Pan and Tiger Lily recognized: not surrender, not bravado, but a compromise that honored both strategy and safety. Their faces were flushed from the cold, eyes bright with the kind of fear that sharpens clarity.

Tiger Lily's shoulders softened just enough for Pan to see it. She turned to the map, her finger tracing the mountain paths. "Send the younger boys with the best archers from the Clan," she said, voice now the cold, steady thing it had been before. "Hide them in the mountain cover—overhangs and caves, places where Hook's men can't easily root them out. Make them invisible. Give them signal fires and horns. They hold. If we make our push left and bait Hook to pursue, the mountain archers pick off reinforcements. They'll be the strike that breaks claws."

Pan's answer was immediate. "We move at first light. I'll lead the left sweep with Tiger Lily and the elder fighters. A smaller, fast-moving element—me and a handful of boys—will cross the ridge to harass and draw. The mountain archers held the kids and injured. If Hook splits, they get cut down."

Tiger Lily's hand hovered over the marked routes, then she tapped the ridge where Pan wanted to send the harassment element. "You'll take the risk," she said quietly. "You'll be exposed. No glorified charge. Small teams. Pick your men. No lone runs."

Pan swallowed, the memory of Bell's wings in his arms squeezing his chest. "No lone runs," he agreed. His voice steadied. "And if it goes wrong—we fall back. The mountain is our refuge, not a grave."

They worked the plan into a scaffold: who went where, how the youngest would be led into the limestone caves by Clan archers at dusk, what signals would mark Hook's movement (three low horns for a pullback, two quick whistles for immediate retreat), the staggered timing so the flanking force met the lagoon at the same moment the mountain archers opened fire. Tiger Lily set contingencies—fallback lines, caches of herbs and water in the caves, a healer's tent hidden behind a boulder near the ridge for emergencies. Pan added an element of deception—false tracks and decoy camps to bait scouts away from the real mountain entrances.

When the orders were finally set, Pan felt a hollow tightness in his gut—the cost of compromise and command. It spread them thinner than either had liked, but the plan covered both routes and, most importantly, it kept the children and the wounded in the most defensible ground they had.

They called the boys together. In a flurry of hushed movements and clipped commands the roster filled: youngest boys and the Clan's three best archers—Maru, Sela, and Old Ivo—were assigned to the mountains. A dozen steady hands and the best slingers would accompany the archers to set up perches and snares. Tiger Lily picked the men she trusted most to watch the caves and tend the wounded. Pan chose his runners—quick, silent—who would relay signals between ridge and lagoon.

"Remember," Tiger Lily said to the younger boys before they slipped away under the cloak of evening mist, her voice somehow both stern and warm, "hide in shadow. Hunt by hush. Protect one another. Do not leave the caves unless you hear three low horns."

The boys nodded, fear sharpening into purpose. They crept from the tent in a small, resolute column, lanterns snuffed, cloaks pulled tight, moving toward the mountain's mouth like ghosts. Pan walked them to the first turn in the path, kneeling to meet each of their eyes. "You watch the world for us," he said softly. "You keep the songs safe. You keep Bell safe. If anything happens, you yell. We come."

They left with the careful stealth of those who know what matters—life, family, the small and fragile things at the heart of their world. As the tent flap fell closed, Tiger Lily and Pan lingered a moment over the map, both of them taller now in different ways: she in her steady resolve, he in the tempered clarity that only hard lessons give.

Outside, the night slid its dark hand across the camp. The plan was set, awkward and dangerous and right. The forest listened; Hook's scouts watched. Somewhere beyond the trees, the captain tested patience like a blade against leather. Inside the tent, Pan and Tiger Lily sealed the course of the next move—two leaders who had argued, clashed, and finally found a way to protect the children by covering both choices at once.

Chapter 36: The Last Light of the Forest

Dawn broke slowly and uncertainly, filtering through the canopy like spilled gold. The forest held its breath, caught between storm and silence, between what was and what would come. The camp beneath Hangman's Tree stirred with quiet purpose—voices low, the shuffle of boots, the clink of metal and glass, the whisper of fabric being tied, secured, packed. The Lost Boys moved with a tense energy that made even the air feel brittle, every movement careful, deliberate. They had done this before, countless times, but this morning carried a gravity that none of them could shake.

Pan tightened the straps on his pack, the leather stiff from rain and wear, before slinging it across his shoulder. The weight settled against his back like memory. His fingers brushed the carved wood of his flute tucked inside—a token of a simpler time, a reminder of who he had once been. He adjusted the dagger at his hip, the one Hook had forged and lost long ago, and exhaled slowly through his nose.

Outside his tent, the camp was a storm of motion. Boys hurried to and fro, their laughter forced, their nerves barely hidden. Clan warriors moved among them, their quiet discipline bringing a kind of order to the chaos.

Pan passed by small knots of preparation—two boys arguing over rations, another testing the string of his bow with trembling fingers, Tiger Lily kneeling over the map one final time with the elder scouts.

Pan crouched now and then to tie a strap, tighten a pack, fix a buckle that a boy's shaking hands couldn't manage. He murmured words of encouragement, steady and soft, the tone of an older brother rather than a commander. Each glance, each small touch, reminded him of why they fought—why he couldn't afford another reckless mistake.

But even with the bustle, his mind kept circling back to one place—the healer's tent.

He hesitated before pushing through the flap, his chest tightening at the hush that greeted him. The tent smelled of herbs and faint smoke, of rain-damp earth and the metallic scent of magic half-spent. Light filtered through the canvas walls in muted gold, catching on the lingering motes that still drifted in the air like tiny suns.

Bell lay at the center of it all, her small frame resting in a bed of moss and woven silk. Her wings—once brilliant with the sheen of dawn—now shimmered only faintly, their edges dimming like the last embers of a dying fire. The faint pulse of golden light at her chest flickered weakly, a fragile rhythm barely holding. She looked peaceful, too still, as though any sudden noise might shatter her entirely.

Pan knelt beside her, his knees pressing into the damp earth. He reached out, but stopped just short of touching her, afraid the warmth of his hand might disrupt what little magic kept her tethered to the world.

"Hey, Bells," he whispered, voice cracking on the nickname. "The boys are ready. Even the little ones." His throat tightened. "You'd be proud. You always are."

The silence of the tent seemed to fold around him, heavy, listening.

Pan swallowed hard, eyes flicking over the soft flicker of her light. "They say you'll pull through. You always do. But..." He exhaled, slow and trembling. "If you can hear me, I want you to know—I'm sorry. For everything that happened. For what I didn't see coming."

His hand found her fingers, cool and weightless in his palm. "You told me once that Neverland was alive because we believed in it. Because you believed in us." His voice dropped, a rough whisper. "So don't stop now, yeah? Don't stop believing. I need you here when it's over."

He leaned closer, forehead almost brushing hers, the faint hum of magic whispering between them. "I promise you, Bell. I'll keep them safe. The boys, the clan, all of them. I won't lose another one. I'll make it right."

The promise lodged deep, heavy and electric, and before he could second-guess it, he pressed his lips gently to hers—a kiss that tasted of earth, salt, and everything left unsaid. A whisper of gold flared from her chest, faint but real, like a heartbeat answering from far away.

Pan drew back, blinking hard, a breath catching in his throat. He brushed his thumb over her hand once more and then stood. "I'll be back," he said softly. "You hold on, Bells. You wait for me."

Outside, the camp was almost ready. The healers packed their remaining herbs and talismans, preparing to leave with the archers and the younger boys heading into the mountains. The oldest healer, her eyes ancient and knowing, met Pan's gaze as he stepped out.

"She will stay here," she said quietly, her tone not a question but a promise. "We will guard her, as you asked. If the winds shift, we will send word."

Pan nodded. "Keep her safe. Whatever it takes."

The healer inclined her head, then turned back into the tent, the golden light spilling briefly before the flap fell shut.

Tiger Lily stood near the edge of camp, conferring with the scouts. She turned as Pan approached, her posture all steel and purpose. "The archers are moving out now," she said. "The boys are packed and the caves are ready. The last group leaves within the hour."

"Good," Pan replied, adjusting the strap on his pack. "We move as soon as they're gone. Left around the mountain, through the lower forest paths. Hook's eyes will be on the ridge; we'll come from where he least expects it."

The war horn sounded once—low, resonant, echoing through the trees. A signal.

The mountain group began to depart, the youngest boys and the healers moving in a quiet procession toward the mist-covered slopes. Pan watched them go, his chest aching as he saw Curly glance back, give a small, determined nod. He returned it with a faint smile, proud and afraid all at once.

When the last of them had vanished into the gray, Pan turned to the remaining warriors—the boys, the Clan, Tiger Lily at their head. The air smelled of moss and iron, of dawn about to break open into battle.

"Let's move," Pan called, his voice firm, carrying over the camp. "Stay low, stay sharp, and watch each other's backs. We make for the forest line before the sun breaks. No noise until we reach the lagoon's edge."

The group began to move, the sound of boots on wet earth muffled under the heavy canopy. Pan took one last glance back—the hollow trunk of Hangman's Tree, the faint glow of the healer's tent like a lantern in the dark—and then turned away, leading them into the forest.

The mist swallowed them as they went, the trees whispering their farewells. Somewhere behind, in the hush of the tent, Bell's light flickered once more—a faint, golden pulse that lingered in the dawn.

Chapter 37: The Language of Goodbyes

The march began before the sun had fully risen. The forest was drenched in mist, every step swallowed by the damp hush that clung to the ground. Pan led from the front, his boots sinking into soft earth, every sense alert. Around him, the boys and the warriors of Le Clan de L'Aura Radieuse moved in near silence, their breaths forming pale ghosts in the cold morning air.

The sound of distant gulls carried from the coast—the faintest echo of the lagoon they approached—but beneath that was something else. A rhythm. A pulse. The kind of silence that wasn't natural.

Tiger Lily's hand brushed the hilt of her blade as she walked beside him. "Something's wrong," she murmured, eyes flicking to the canopy above.

Pan nodded once, jaw tight. "I know. They're close."

And then it came.

The first sound—a single snap of a branch—was followed by a rush of movement. Shadows burst from the mist, Hook's men pouring from the undergrowth like a tide of ghosts. Steel met steel.

Arrows whistled. The air erupted with the clash of blades and the sharp crack of muskets.

"Form up!" Pan shouted, voice cutting through the chaos. "Hold the line!"

The Lost Boys rallied, forming a loose semicircle around the younger ones. Clan warriors moved like wind and lightning, their painted faces fierce, their movements precise. But Hook's men were relentless, pressing from every side, the smell of gunpowder mixing with the wet scent of moss and iron.

Through the madness, Pan caught a flash of crimson—the edge of Hook's coat glinting through the trees. His chest tightened. It was like seeing a ghost and destiny all at once. The old fear surged, tangled with rage, guilt, and the echo of Bell's pale face in the healer's tent.

He didn't think. He *never* did when it came to Hook.

"HOOK!" Pan's voice tore through the din. "I'll go with you! Just stop this!"

The battle faltered. The gunfire ceased in stuttering bursts until silence rippled outward like a wave. Hook's silhouette emerged slowly through the haze, the long coat dragging through the mud, pistol at his side, his eyes unreadable even in the dim light.

Around Pan, the boys froze. The goons nearest him took the opportunity—rough hands grabbed his shoulders, forcing him to his knees. Tiger Lily shouted his name, stepping forward before being held back by a pair of pirates.

Pan's breath came sharp, wild, his knees sinking into the cold mud as Hook approached. He could feel the weight of every gaze—his boys, the clan, the enemy—resting on him. He could feel their disbelief.

Hook stopped in front of him, boots glinting faintly with water and blood. The older man's expression was calm, almost gentle, but the tension beneath it crackled like a drawn bowstring. Slowly, deliberately, Hook reached down and took Pan's chin between two fingers, forcing him to look up.

Pan met his gaze—unflinching, furious, but something in him trembled. Hook studied him in silence, eyes flicking across his face as if reading every scar, every flicker of emotion. The world seemed to contract around them, sound fading until the forest held its breath.

"Still so stubborn," Hook murmured finally, voice low enough only Pan could hear. "Still pretending you can save everyone."

Pan didn't answer. His jaw flexed under Hook's grip.

Then Hook smiled—small, knowing, and utterly cold. He raised a hand, gesturing to his men. Instantly, the pirates released their hold on the Lost Boys and clan warriors. The hands restraining Pan shoved him forward roughly before stepping back.

Tiger Lily lunged, shouting, "Pan!" but he turned sharply, holding out his hand.

"Veexzchoj takh, zah quoquekioj takh queko. Chea Ttupp Koquoquzok."

The ancient words rolled from his tongue like a spell, heavy and melodic in the air.

Tiger Lily froze mid-step, her expression contorting between fury, confusion, and heartbreak. She knew the tongue—old and sacred, spoken only in rites of departure and remembrance—but the meaning struck her deeper than any blade.

Goodbyes hurt, but memories hurt more. You shall remember.

The forest seemed to shiver at the words, a hush falling so profound that even the birds went silent.

Hook's eyes flicked toward Tiger Lily, then back to Pan. For a moment, something unreadable crossed his face—an emotion too brief to name, perhaps recognition, perhaps regret.

Pan's chest rose and fell, his pulse loud in his ears. He could feel every muscle trembling with restraint, every instinct screaming to draw his blade, to fight, to *end* this. But the faces of the boys behind him, of Tiger Lily, of Bell in the tent—all of it anchored him.

He bowed his head once, a single, deliberate motion, and said through gritted teeth, "You have me. Let them go."

Hook's gaze lingered a heartbeat longer, then he gave a sharp nod. His men hesitated, but when he barked a single order, they began to retreat, melting into the mist as swiftly as they had come.

Pan stood there in the quiet aftermath, mud on his knees, blood in the air, and silence pressing in like a weight. The boys whispered his name. Tiger Lily's breath hitched in disbelief, tears and anger warring on her face.

Hook turned away first, his voice drifting back over his shoulder. "Remember your promise, boy. You're mine now."

And with that, he disappeared into the fog, his men vanishing behind him until the forest was still again.

Pan remained unmoving, his heart pounding in his throat, the echo of Bell's fading light and Tiger Lily's shocked eyes haunting him in equal measure. He had made his choice, and the world felt suddenly smaller for it.

Chapter 38: Tethers in the Storm

The path wound through dripping ferns and twisted roots, the forest closing around them in green-gray shadow. Thunder rolled above like an ancient drum, the heartbeat of Neverland itself. Every step squelched in the sodden earth, and the air reeked of wet moss and gun oil.

Hook moved ahead with the effortless grace of someone who had made the jungle his ally. His coat flared with each stride, dark against the pale mist. Pan trailed close behind, tense and silent, every nerve straining.

"You've grown strong," Hook said over his shoulder, voice low, velvet-dark. "But strength without discipline is dangerous."

"I'm not reckless," Pan bit out.

Hook laughed softly, a sound that slid under Pan's skin like smoke. "You always were." He slowed his pace until they were side by side. "And yet, you keep surviving. Perhaps you learned something from me after all."

Pan's jaw tightened. "I learned what *not* to become."

That earned another quiet chuckle. Hook's hand brushed his arm—a fleeting contact, but deliberate. It wasn't command this time, nor cruelty. It was familiarity, control disguised as care. Pan flinched but didn't pull away.

Rain pattered harder, dripping from the canopy in steady sheets. Hook leaned closer, voice a murmur just above the storm. "You fight me as though you don't understand what I gave you. Every scar on that skin, every instinct that keeps you alive—you owe to me."

Pan's breath caught, anger and something more tangled in his chest. "I owe you nothing."

Hook's smile was thin. "You owe me everything."

They broke through the last of the trees, and the world opened onto the cliffs above Mermaid Lagoon. The sea below churned black and silver, waves hammering the rocks in furious rhythm. Lightning split the sky, painting Hook's face in stark relief—commanding, predatory, almost beautiful in its precision.

Pan's sword hung at his side, his knuckles white. He thought of Bell—her warmth, her light, her laughter—and the memory steadied him.

"You taught me to fight," he said quietly. "But Bell taught me why."

Hook turned toward him fully, eyes narrowing, rain slicking his hair against his brow. "Love?" he asked, almost gently, almost mocking. "That fragile little thing?"

Pan's voice was steady now. "It's the only thing that ever made me stronger than you."

For a moment, silence. Only the storm spoke. Hook's gaze searched Pan's face, sharp and unreadable, and then he smiled—slow, dangerous, admiring.

"Then show me, Peter," he said, stepping closer, the sea crashing behind them. "Show me what love has made of you."

The rain fell harder, drumming on their shoulders, blurring the world into gray and silver. Pan lifted his chin, eyes blazing, his body trembling not from fear but from fury and the weight of everything unspoken between them—loyalty twisted into obsession, mentorship turned to war.

Whatever storm waited beyond the cliffs, he was ready for it.

He would survive Hook.
He would protect Bell.
And Neverland would remember.

Chapter 39: The Devil You Remember

The storm thinned to a restless drizzle by the time they reached the cliffs overlooking Mermaid Lagoon. The sea stretched out beneath them, black and vast, its surface bruised by the storm. Jagged rocks jutted from the foam like the bones of something ancient. Below, the faint glow of lanterns flickered—a constellation of light marking Hook's camp sprawled along the shore.

The ships of the Jolly Roger's fleet rocked against the waves, their black sails slick with rain, their masts creaking like old trees. Pirates moved like shadows between the tents, the muted ring of metal and the low murmur of voices blending with the hiss of the surf. The air smelled of brine, oil, and gunpowder.

Hook descended first, boots sure against the slick stones, his stride easy, confident. He didn't look back to see if Pan followed—he didn't need to. He knew Pan would.

Pan's steps echoed his, slower, cautious. His clothes were soaked through, hair plastered to his brow. Every instinct screamed to run, to vanish into the forest, but he forced himself to stay close. The memory of Bell's dimming light—her wings faltering, her breath shallow—burned behind his eyes. *He's the key,* Pan told himself. *End Hook, end this war.*

The camp stilled as they entered. Every pirate that saw him—mud-smeared, rain-soaked, but unbroken—whispered his name like a curse and a legend all at once.

Hook raised a hand, silencing them. "He's under my protection," he said simply. "No one touches him."

The men obeyed. Of course they did.

Inside the largest tent, the air was thick with heat from a brazier and the sharp scent of rum. Maps lay unfurled on the table—tattered, stained, annotated with Hook's meticulous hand. The ink gleamed like spilled blood under the lanternlight.

Hook removed his coat, hanging it carefully on a post before pouring himself a drink. "Still play the leader, do you?" he asked lightly, without turning. "You never learned how heavy that crown becomes when it starts to crack."

Pan didn't answer. His eyes darted to the maps—Neverland's coasts, the mountain passes, the Lagoon's depths drawn with surgical precision. His heart kicked at the sight of markings that stretched all the way to the Redieuse territory. Hook had been planning this for months. Maybe years.

"You think this is about you," Pan said, forcing steadiness into his voice.

Hook's laugh was quiet, dangerous. "Everything here is about you."

He turned, glass in hand, eyes gleaming. "Every choice you make defines this island. Every spark of rebellion feeds it. You and I—we are its heartbeats. Do you still not understand?"

Pan's chest tightened. "You're not Neverland."

"Neither are you," Hook said softly, almost tenderly. "You're just the part of it that refuses to grow up."

The words cut deep, and Hook saw it. He always saw it.

Hook moved closer, the sound of the rain muffled by canvas and wind. "Tell me, Peter. When she dies—your little fairy—what then? Who will you be when there's no one left to believe you're good?"

Pan's breath caught, fury igniting in his chest. He lunged forward, grabbing Hook by the collar, the two of them nose-to-nose. "She's not going to die," Pan growled. "You don't get to say her name."

Hook didn't flinch. He only smiled, slow and cold, one hand rising to rest lightly against Pan's wrist. Not to pry it away—just to remind him who still held the upper hand.

"Anger suits you," Hook murmured. "It's the one thing you've never learned to control."

Pan shoved him back, chest heaving. "You want control? You'll choke on it."

Hook's grin widened, dark and knowing. "Oh, I already have, my boy. That's why I know its taste so well."

For a moment, neither spoke. The air between them crackled like the aftermath of lightning—charged, dangerous, too close to something that felt like recognition.

Outside, thunder rolled again, distant but persistent. Hook turned back to the table, tracing a line across the map with one gloved finger. "You'll stay here tonight," he said. "My men will watch the borders. Tomorrow, I'll show you what real strategy looks like."

Pan's hand twitched toward his sword. "You think I'll follow your orders?"

Hook looked up, meeting his gaze, eyes glinting like the sea under lightning. "You already are."

Pan said nothing. He could feel the weight of the camp pressing in—the guards outside, the hum of the storm, the scent of iron and smoke. Every instinct screamed to act, to strike, to run. But something in Hook's words—his certainty—rooted him where he stood.

Hook poured a second glass and set it on the table beside him. The gesture was subtle, an invitation wrapped in challenge.

"Drink," he said softly. "You'll need it."

Pan hesitated, then stepped forward, the rain still dripping from his hair, his jaw set. He picked up the glass, eyes never leaving Hook's.

The rum burned down his throat like fire. Hook's smile was small, approving.

Outside, lightning flashed again, silhouetting their forms in stark relief against the canvas. Two figures—rivals, reflections, teacher and student—standing on the brink of a storm that would either forge or destroy them both.

And somewhere, far beyond the cliffs and the sea, a faint shimmer flickered through the mist—Bell's magic, weak but alive. A single light refusing to fade.

Pan set the glass down slowly. His voice, when he spoke, was low and certain.
 "When this ends," he said, "you'll see how much I've learned from you."

Hook's smirk deepened. "That's what I'm counting on."

Chapter 40: The Whisper Beneath the Waves

Night had swallowed the lagoon. Only the occasional flash of lightning broke the dark, revealing the jagged skeletons of ships and the shimmer of rain cascading down the masts like silver threads. The storm had quieted, but something in the air still felt charged—alive, waiting.

Pan lay on a cot inside one of Hook's tents, staring at the faint outline of the canvas ceiling. The camp outside had gone mostly still, save for the quiet murmur of guards and the dull rhythm of waves against the rocks. He hadn't slept. He couldn't. Every time he closed his eyes, he saw Bell—the soft gold flicker of her wings dimming beneath his hands, the faint tremor in her breath.

He sat up, every movement deliberate. The rain had slowed to a whisper, and the guards outside the tent were quieter now, lulled by exhaustion and rum. Hook had underestimated how well Pan knew the rhythms of men. Pirates weren't soldiers—they were beasts of habit. And habit made them predictable.

Pan pulled his coat tight and slipped out into the night.

The camp was a labyrinth of shadows and dying firelight. He moved between the tents, keeping low, every sense sharp. He could hear the murmur of the tide below, the faint creak of the Jolly Roger moored at the edge of the lagoon—and then, voices.

Hook's.

Pan froze, his pulse quickening. The sound came from the command tent—the largest one, lit dimly from within by a lantern's flicker. He crept closer, keeping to the canvas walls, until the words came clearer, carried on the salt-heavy air.

"—You've mapped it all wrong, Smee. The fractures run deeper than that. The island's heart doesn't just bleed—it sings when it's breaking."

Pan pressed closer, breath shallow.

Smee's voice came, nervous and rough. "Beggin' your pardon, Cap'n, but we've taken every reading you asked. The tremors near the falls, the shifts in the cliffs—they're worse than before. You sure you want to keep diggin'? It's makin' the island unstable."

"Good," Hook said.

The word landed like a blade.

Pan's brow furrowed. He leaned nearer, careful not to disturb the tent wall.

Hook continued, tone almost reverent. "Neverland thrives on imbalance. It's a place that feeds on imagination, chaos, and memory. Every story has a root—and if I can carve mine deep enough into the island's heart, it will no longer answer to *him*."

Smee hesitated. "You mean the boy."

Hook's voice dropped to a dangerous calm. "I mean the *island itself*. The boy is just its shadow. He'll break when it does."

Pan's stomach twisted.

He'd always known Hook wanted power—wanted revenge—but this was different. This was *destruction*. The kind that would swallow everything, even the things Hook claimed to love.

Smee shuffled, uneasy. "And what of the fairies, Cap'n? The clans won't stand by while we tear into their sacred ground."

"The fairies are dying," Hook said, almost absently. "Their magic fades. The clans will either bow, or burn."

Pan's hand clenched around his dagger. The image of Bell's fading light burned behind his eyes again.

He's killing the island to kill me.

Hook's voice softened, contemplative. "The island bends to belief. Once, it believed in him. Now, it will remember me."

There was a long pause—the sound of Hook pouring another drink, the soft glug of rum hitting glass. Then:

"And when I'm done, Neverland will never again be a playground for children. It will be a kingdom—for those who have earned it."

Pan pulled back slowly, heart hammering. His breath came quickly, ragged.

He needed to get out—needed to warn Tiger Lily, the boys, the archers. But how? The guards were everywhere, and Hook's men had the high ground.

He turned toward the dark ridge beyond the camp. The mountains loomed far in the distance, their peaks ghostlike against the clouded sky. Somewhere up there, the archers watched and waited for a signal that might never come.

Pan reached into his satchel, pulling out a small shard of obsidian—fairy-forged, a gift from Bell when he was younger. When struck, it reflected light farther than fire or mirror could carry. A flare of pure magic—brief, but bright enough to reach the mountains.

He hesitated, thumb brushing its rough edge. If he used it, Hook's men might see too. But if he didn't…

He gritted his teeth. *Bell would've done it without thinking.*

Pan crouched low behind a row of barrels, pulling two flint stones from his belt. He struck them together, hard. Sparks flew—and when one hit the shard, it erupted in a brief pulse of blue light, sharp and clean as moonfire.

He covered it quickly, pressing it to his chest, whispering under his breath, "Come on, come on…"

High above the lagoon, a faint answering flicker gleamed from the mountainside—a signal returned. The archers had seen.

Pan exhaled a shaky breath. For a heartbeat, relief threatened to take him.

Then—

"Beautiful trick," came Hook's voice from the darkness.

Pan froze.

The captain stood a few feet away, cloak half-drawn, his pistol gleaming faintly in the lanternlight. His expression wasn't angry. It was *amused.*

"Firelight from stone," Hook murmured. "You really are your mother's son."

Pan turned, forcing defiance into his stance despite the tremor in his limbs. "You talk too much."

Hook stepped closer, boots silent in the mud. "And you listen too well."

Their eyes met—one burning with fury, the other with cold fascination.

Hook's smile was slow, deliberate. "Go on, then. Run to your little army. Warn them. Tell them the island's bleeding—and that the boy who never grew up is the one who made it bleed first."

Pan didn't answer. He turned and bolted into the forest, Hook's laughter echoing behind him, low and certain as thunder.

Chapter 41: Flight and Fire

The forest swallowed him.

Pan's boots sank into mud churned by the rain, roots and fallen branches threatening to trip him with every step. Leaves clung to his clothes, slick and heavy, and the wind whispered through the trees like a warning. His lungs burned, heart hammering—not just from exertion, but from the revelation he carried. Hook wasn't after him alone. Hook was after the *island*.

Every shadow seemed alive, every sound a possible threat. But Pan didn't slow. He had to reach the mountains before dawn, before Hook could make the next move.

Behind him, faintly, he could hear the camp—Hook's laughter still echoing in the distance, a dark lullaby that twisted through the night air. Pan pressed on, muscles screaming, mind spinning. He had to warn the archers. He had to protect the children. He had to protect Bell.

The first ridge appeared just as the sky lightened, gray and restless with the remnants of the storm. Pan scrambled up the slick stones, hands clutching at roots and jagged rocks, the shards of obsidian in his satchel vibrating faintly against his chest—a tether to the magic he'd sent earlier. The signal had worked; they knew he was coming.

Panting, he reached the summit. The wind tore at him, whipping rain and mist across his soaked face. And there they were—the archers from the clan, stationed in hiding among the crags, bows strung, eyes sharp, watching the forest below.

Tiger Lily stepped forward from the shadows, her face streaked with rain, eyes blazing with fierce relief. "Peter!" she cried. "You made it!"

Pan skidded to a stop, sinking to his knees for a moment, catching his breath. "I… I overheard," he gasped, voice ragged. "Hook isn't just after me. He's—he's going after the island. The whole thing. He plans to destroy… everything."

The archers exchanged worried glances, murmuring low among themselves. Tiger Lily's jaw tightened. "He'll burn us all if we give him the chance," she said, voice low and steady. "We have to move, warn the boys, get the children to safety."

Pan nodded, hands shaking, still catching his breath. "The signal worked. They know we're coming." His fingers brushed the flint shard in his satchel. "But we have to act fast. Hook won't wait."

The younger boys, already huddled with the best archers from the clan, shifted nervously under their blankets and moss, eyes wide as they peered over the rocks. Pan's chest tightened at the thought of them in danger. He swallowed hard. *Bell is weak… the kids are vulnerable… I can't fail.*

Tiger Lily crouched beside him, gripping his shoulder. "You're not alone, Peter. You have all of us. Now, tell me everything you heard—every word. No details spared. We need to know how to stop him."

Pan recounted Hook's plan, voice low and tense, trembling with anger and fear. Every word seemed to weigh heavier than the last: destabilizing the island, bending its magic, using its power to fuel his own rise. The archers' faces darkened, bows tightening, quivers shifting with renewed urgency.

When he finished, Tiger Lily exhaled slowly. "Then we do both. We protect the children, and we hit Hook where it hurts." She turned toward the archers. "Spread out. The younger boys stay here. Use the mountains' cover to shield them. Everyone else—flank to the left of the Lagoon. Cut off his men before they reach the water."

Pan rose to his feet, body still trembling from the flight and revelation. His eyes scanned the horizon where the dark waters of Mermaid Lagoon churned beneath the storm-soaked sky. "It'll be risky," he muttered. "It spreads us thin—but at least the kids will be safe, and Bell… Bell will survive."

Tiger Lily's gaze met his, sharp and commanding. "Then lead them, Peter. Use what Hook taught you—but don't let him teach you *fear*. The boys trust you. So do I."

Pan's hands clenched into fists, sword at his side, resolve hardening. "Then we do it. We will stop him tonight. We stop him for the island, for the children, for Bell."

He cast one last glance at the mountainside, where the archers and younger boys huddled in the rocks, their faces pale but determined. The shard in his satchel pulsed faintly, a reminder that magic was still alive in Neverland, still on their side.

The march began—quiet at first, stealthy, through mud and mist, every footstep measured. The shadows stretched long beneath the canopy, bending to their will. Pan's mind raced, every strategy he'd learned under Hook and through his years with the Lost Boys twisting into a single, coherent purpose: strike fast, protect the weak, and bring the fight to the captain before he could shatter the island.

The first signs of Hook's scouts appeared just as dawn broke. Mist clung to the underbrush like fingers, hiding movement until it was too late. Pan gestured sharply, signaling the archers to hold their fire, waiting for the precise moment.

"Stay low," he whispered, voice cutting through the fog. "Wait for my mark."

The archers obeyed. Tiger Lily's hand found his shoulder briefly, grounding him. Pan inhaled, sword tight in his grip, pulse thrumming. The storm inside him—the terror, the anger, the guilt over Bell—was coiled, ready to spring.

Tonight, the fight began in earnest. And for the first time in weeks, Pan felt the heavy weight of purpose replace the chaotic fear that had haunted him since Hook first appeared.

He would protect the island. He would protect Bell. He would not fail.

The shadows shifted. Hook's men were coming.

Chapter 42: The First Clash

Mist clung to the forest like a living veil, curling around roots and rocks, hiding movement and muffling sound. Pan led the group down a narrow pass along the mountainside, the Lost Boys flanking to his left, Tiger Lily at his right, archers hidden above in the jagged rocks. Every shadow could conceal an enemy, every snapping twig a signal of Hook's advance.

"Keep your heads low!" Pan hissed, voice barely more than a whisper. "Wait for the signal. Do *not* engage until I give the mark."

Tiger Lily's eyes narrowed. "Peter, you need to stay focused. Do not—"

"Quiet!" Pan snapped, frustration sharp and dangerous. The memory of Bell—her pale wings, the pulse of magic fading under the healers' hands—tightened like a knot in his chest. He *wouldn't* let anyone else get hurt on his watch. Not now. Not ever.

Ahead, movement rippled through the trees. Hook's men were already in position, silhouettes blending with the forest shadows. They carried muskets, cutlasses glinting faintly as they moved, and Pan's pulse surged.

Without thinking, he sprinted forward, leaving Tiger Lily's hand half-raised in warning. His sword flashed in the dim light, and he called out: "Hook! I'm coming!"

Chaos erupted.

The archers above released a hail of arrows, forcing Hook's scouts to scatter. Lost Boys yelled as they scrambled to engage, but Pan had gone too far ahead. He leapt into the first cluster of enemy soldiers, swinging with precision and reckless strength, eyes locked on the distant glint of Hook's coat.

"Peter! Stop!" Tiger Lily yelled, dashing after him. "You're spreading us too thin!"

But Pan was beyond reason. He *had* to face Hook. He *had* to stop him before more of Neverland's magic—more of Bell's life—was at risk. His swings were brutal, quick, precise, but the men were many, and for every one he felled, two more appeared.

Tiger Lily reached him just as a musket flared nearby, the report echoing off the cliffs. She slammed her hand against Pan's chest, forcing him back. "*Enough!*"

Pan's chest heaved, sweat and rain dripping into his eyes. "I… I can take him! I *have* to!"

"You're reckless!" she snapped, eyes blazing. "I will not let you die because of a single obsession! You're supposed to *lead*!"

The soldiers regrouped, forming a tight line, and for a heartbeat Pan froze. Hook's shadow loomed beyond the mist, pistol in hand, studying him, eyes flicking with amusement and assessment.

Pan's knees hit the forest floor as the enemy forced him down, the line of pirates pressing him back while Tiger Lily pulled him further from Hook's reach. He fought the urge to leap forward again, to charge straight at the man who had haunted him since his earliest lessons, to strike a final blow that could either save everything or doom it.

Hook's gaze swept over him, slow and deliberate, lingering with that predator's patience Pan knew too well. He raised a hand, and the pirates hesitated—Hook's silent command radiating control.

Tiger Lily's grip on Pan's arm tightened, her voice harsh but steady. "Peter! Focus. *This is not just about him. It's about all of us.* You'll have your chance, but not like this."

Pan exhaled sharply, body trembling, the adrenaline twisting into guilt. He glanced at the boys—huddled, fighting back to back, faces pale but resolute. His own impulsiveness had nearly cost them everything.

Hook's smirk deepened. He was enjoying it—the struggle, the restraint breaking and reforming, the boy wrestling with the dangerous cocktail of courage and fury. He didn't fire. Not yet. He simply observed, testing Pan's limits, savoring the lesson in restraint he always demanded.

Tiger Lily shoved him toward cover. "Move! The archers will protect the young ones. *You* need to lead them safely. This isn't your fight alone, Peter."

Pan's throat tightened. He wanted to argue, to defy, to leap forward into Hook's waiting line. But the memory of Bell—the fading pulse of her wings, the healers working tirelessly—anchored him.

He lowered himself to the ground, chest heaving, eyes sweeping the battlefield. The archers above released another volley of arrows, cutting down more of Hook's men. The Lost Boys pushed forward, disciplined and united now under Pan's regained clarity.

Pan finally found his voice, directing the movements of his group, combining the lessons of Hook's brutal training with the loyalty and ingenuity of the Lost Boys. Orders flew, arrows struck, swords clashed—the forest alive with motion, chaos, and strategy.

For the first time since Bell's injury, Pan felt control. Not complete control—but enough to channel his reckless energy into something *purposeful*. He could protect the children, the archers, the boys, and Bell. And he could still stop Hook. But only if he tempered his fury with patience.

Hook retreated into the shadows, pistol lowered but still watching, letting Pan's group believe they had gained the advantage. The real lesson wasn't over. Pan knew that.

But for now... for the first time in hours, he *breathed*.

And the forest, soaked with rain and echoing with the cries of battle, waited for the next move.

Chapter 43: Counterstrike

The forest had quieted, though the tension was electric, vibrating through every leaf and root. Rain still slicked the branches, dripping in slow, rhythmic taps that mirrored Pan's pulse. He crouched behind a fallen log, surveying the battlefield below with Tiger Lily at his side, the Lost Boys regrouping and the archers perched high in the rocky crags.

Pan's chest heaved, not from exertion this time, but from the weight of responsibility pressing down on him. Bell's face flashed in his mind—pale, her wings dimming under the healers' magic—and the memory of her vulnerability burned him with guilt. Every impulsive choice had brought them here. Every reckless charge had risked her life. He would *not* let it happen again.

"Peter," Tiger Lily said, voice quiet but firm, pulling him from his spiraling thoughts. "We need a plan. They'll come back, and stronger. What's our next move?"

Pan nodded, jaw tight. "The archers are in the mountains. They'll cover the younger boys and the injured. We can't risk them in the front line." His eyes flicked toward the craggy peaks where the children huddled behind Tiger Lily's most skilled archers. "We flank Hook's men from the left, just like we practiced—but we'll coordinate with the archers above. Timing is everything. Wait for my signal."

Tiger Lily's gaze met his, searching, measuring the weight of his command. "You're taking responsibility for all of this... again," she said, almost softly. "Don't let your anger cloud your judgment."

"I won't," Pan muttered, though the tremor in his hands betrayed him. "I... I have to do this *right*."

They poured over the map together in the makeshift war tent—a sheet of leather stretched over logs, inked with trails and positions. Pan traced the route over the mountains, Tiger Lily insisting they should skirt left of the lagoon, using the trees for cover. The argument ran long, voices low but sharp, each refusing to yield.

Finally, the boys who had fought in the first skirmish entered the tent, breathless and dripping, adding their own perspective. "Both routes work," one said. "If we split, we cover the archers and the younger boys, and we can still cut off Hook's men from behind."

Pan's shoulders relaxed slightly. "Then we do it. Archers and children stay in the mountains. The rest of us flank left of the lagoon. We hit fast and precisely." He drew in a deep breath. "We protect what matters, and we hit Hook where it hurts most—his pride, his control."

Tiger Lily nodded, placing a firm hand on his shoulder. "Then let's move."

The march was tense, silent, with only the drip of rain and the occasional rustle of leaves breaking the quiet. Pan led the Lost Boys along the muddy trail, Tiger Lily beside him, watching every shadow for movement. Ahead, the water of Mermaid Lagoon reflected the gray, storm-laden sky. The enemy could be anywhere, waiting.

Then, faintly, movement in the trees—Hook's scouts.

Pan signaled to the archers hidden in the peaks. A volley of arrows rained down, forcing the scouts to scatter. The Lost Boys surged forward in disciplined formation, swords drawn, shields clashing against Hook's men as the ambush ignited.

Pan's pulse jumped, the adrenaline mixing with fear and guilt. He had to lead, had to make up for the mistakes earlier. Every strike, every command, every strategic move was precise, honed by both Hook's brutal lessons and his own growing intuition.

Tiger Lily stayed close, intercepting a pirate who tried to flank Pan. "You're better than yesterday!" she yelled, voice sharp and steady. "Focus, Peter!"

The archers fired from above, arrows cutting through the mist. The younger boys, huddled safely under their cover, gasped in awe, watching the coordinated assault unfold. Pan's heart clenched—not with pride, but with the overwhelming need to *keep everyone safe.*

Hook's men were pushed back, forced to regroup, giving Pan and Tiger Lily the moment they needed to communicate silently with the archers. Signals flickered across the rocky crags: the timing, the angles, the retreat points. The mountains became a fortress, the children shielded from the chaos below.

Pan's mind raced. He could *feel* Hook's gaze, calculating, predicting, waiting for the first sign of weakness. But Pan had learned restraint—learned the cost of reckless impulsiveness. He channeled every lesson, every scar, every loss into focus, guiding the boys, directing the archers, coordinating every move.

And still, in the back of his mind, Bell's face hovered—fragile, magical, a tether keeping him grounded. He whispered a silent promise to her: *I will keep them safe. I will not fail.*

As the first wave of Hook's men was pushed back toward the lagoon, Pan knew this was only the beginning. The battle would escalate, Hook's cunning would force them to adapt, and the island itself hung in peril.

But for now, in this fleeting calm, strategy and loyalty aligned. Pan's reckless fury had been tempered, honed into leadership. And though the storm of battle was far from over, he felt the first flicker of hope: they could survive. They *would* survive.

And Bell... Bell would still have a chance.

Chapter 44: Ascension to the Ship

The flanking maneuver had begun before dawn, the mist still hanging thick in the gorge like a living curtain. Pan and Tiger Lily moved with the Lost Boys and the clan's warriors, pressing left of Mermaid Lagoon as planned.

Every step was deliberate, every movement choreographed in the rhythm of battle. The archers above had the younger boys and injured hidden in the mountains, a hail of arrows providing both cover and deadly warning for any enemy scout who dared stray.

Pan's pulse raced, but this time it was disciplined. His sword flashed in the pale light as he directed the troops, every command sharp, every order precise. The pirates, surprised by the coordination and precision of the flanking force, struggled to regroup. Spears and cutlasses clashed, but Pan's group pushed forward with an unyielding momentum, the chorus of battle cries echoing across the gorge.

Tiger Lily moved like a shadow, a whirlwind of motion beside Pan. Her elite guards cleared a path, and the Lost Boys surged in formation, cutting off the enemy's retreat and driving them toward the riverbank.

The cacophony of war—shouts, clashing steel, and the metallic tang of blood—was almost drowned out by the sound of the wind rising, carrying the telltale hum of sails above.

"There!" Pan pointed, eyes narrowing. Hook's ship hovered impossibly above the gorge, suspended as if the storm itself obeyed him. "We go up. Now."

Tiger Lily's guards immediately formed a support line, swinging thick ropes over the cliff edges and pulling Pan and her forward. With a leap of faith, Pan gripped her hand, and together they were hoisted upward, the Lost Boys and clan warriors covering their ascent with arrows and swinging blades. The wind whipped around them, tangling hair and clothing, but Pan's eyes burned with a singular focus—Hook.

When their boots hit the deck, the scene that greeted them was worse than anything Pan had imagined.

Hook stood over a massive, ancient creature of Neverland, its glittering scales and crystalline eyes dulled by pain. Its limbs twisted unnaturally as Hook's teeth sank deep into its chest, magical energy thrumming violently as it was drained from the creature. The sickening sound of bones snapping echoed across the deck, mingling with the creature's last, ragged breaths. Hook exhaled slowly, a grotesque satisfaction curling the corners of his lips.

Pan froze for a heartbeat, stomach roiling with disbelief. All this time... this was his plan? Sucking Neverland dry to maintain his strength, his youth, his immortality. Rage ignited, a wildfire in his chest, consuming strategy, reason, and fear.

Every betrayal, every innocent harmed, every moment Hook had spent twisting Neverland to his will pressed down on Pan like a physical weight. Bell's pale wings flashed before his eyes, the children in the mountains, the Lost Boys, the clan, the creatures Hook had tortured—all of it fueled a fury that churned hotter with each passing second. The world around him blurred; he could feel Hook's smug triumph in the air, and it only fed the storm rising inside him.

Before Hook could speak, before the monstrous explanation could reach Pan's ears, his hand moved of its own accord. Sword unsheathed in a blur of silver and steel, Pan's movements precise, furious, unstoppable. Every fiber of his being screamed, every ounce of betrayal and grief translating into lethal force.

He drove the blade through Hook's throat, the sound of tearing flesh cutting through the chaos of the storm above the gorge. For a fleeting heartbeat, Pan felt the full, unchained weight of his anger, a dark, burning satisfaction that this betrayal would no longer haunt Neverland—or him.

Hook's eyes widened, a mixture of shock, disbelief, and the faintest trace of admiration mingling with the crimson spilling across his collar. His hands clawed at Pan's arm for a fleeting second, but it was too late. Pan's grip was iron, his teeth clenched, every ounce of rage and heartbreak focused into the single act of vengeance.

Pan stood over Hook, chest heaving, eyes blazing with fury. He watched the life drain from the man who had been mentor, tormentor, and shadow to his entire existence. For the creatures Hook had killed, the blood spilled across Neverland, the boys he had endangered, the clan he had mocked, and the fragile, healing light of Bell—Pan let his rage claim the moment entirely.

Hook choked, clawing at the deck, struggling for breath that would not come. Pan's gaze did not waver; he did not flinch. The years of manipulation, the lessons twisted by obsession, the terror and desire—everything culminated here, in the throbbing heat of justice and retribution.

Tiger Lily's hand gripped Pan's shoulder, grounding him, whispering urgently, "Peter… enough. We can't stay here."

Pan's chest heaved as he let the sword fall, blood and rain mixing on the deck. He didn't look away from Hook, didn't let the victory feel triumphant. Instead, his body quaked with the enormity of what he'd done, the personal, raw weight of vengeance.

The storm above the gorge seemed to pause in reverent silence, acknowledging the death of the man who had tormented Neverland for decades.

He turned slowly toward Tiger Lily, toward the remaining boys and clan members, and exhaled—a long, shaky release of rage, grief, and relief. Bell's face lingered in his mind, a promise tethering him to sanity.

"We move," Pan said, voice low, resolute. "We make sure *everything* he wanted to destroy… survives. Neverland survives."

Tiger Lily nodded, hand tightening around his arm, guiding him toward the ropes that would bring them back down from the hovering ship. The Lost Boys rallied behind them, eyes wide but trusting, ready to follow Pan wherever the tide of battle—and his newfound clarity—would take them.

Above the gorge, the storm swirled, echoing the tension still coiled within Pan—but for the first time, he moved with purpose, tempered by rage, tempered by love, and tempered by the knowledge that some lessons, however cruel, had finally been learned.

Chapter 45: The Weight of Victory

The ropes swayed violently in the wind as Pan and Tiger Lily guided the Lost Boys down from Hook's hovering ship. Rain plastered their hair and drenched their clothing, dripping from every edge of the forest canopy. The gorge below was a chaotic jumble of mist, mud, and the groaning of Hook's defeated forces retreating in confusion.

Pan's hands trembled slightly as he landed on solid ground, sword still slick with blood, though his mind was not on the gore. His thoughts were a tangle of rage, guilt, and relief—an emotional storm that refused to settle. Tiger Lily's hand remained on his shoulder, firm and grounding, but even her presence could not fully steady the roiling chaos inside him.

"Bell," he whispered to himself, his voice rough and hoarse. The memory of her wings, dimmed yet flickering with faint magic, pulled him forward like gravity. The archers had already escorted the children and the injured back into the mountains. Pan's focus was singular: reach the healers' tent and make sure Bell survived this night.

The tent was quiet except for the soft murmurs of magic, the crackle of energy weaving through the air as the elder healer hovered over Bell. Her chest rose and fell slowly, color returning to her cheeks, her wings glimmering faintly despite exhaustion. Pan dropped to his knees beside her, hands shaking as he brushed wet strands of hair from her face.

"I… I promised," he murmured, voice breaking. "I promised I'd keep you safe." His thumb traced the edge of her cheek, lingering over the warmth that remained despite her weakened state. "I—I did it. I made sure… we survived."

The healer's eyes flicked up at him, then returned to Bell, murmuring softly, reinforcing the magic, strengthening the fragile tether keeping her alive. Pan's chest tightened with relief, and for a heartbeat, he allowed himself to feel the fragility of life, of magic, of the world they were fighting to protect.

Tiger Lily stepped closer, her expression sharp. "Peter…" she said, her voice low but firm, "you killed him."

"I had to," Pan admitted, voice trembling. "For everything. For the creatures, the boys, the clan… for Bell." He clenched his fists, nails digging into his palms, struggling to contain the flood of emotions threatening to pull him under. "I couldn't let him… ever do this again."

Tiger Lily's gaze softened slightly but did not waver. "You acted impulsively," she said. "As you always do. But you tempered it this time with strategy. You led them, coordinated the flanking, ensured the archers were safe… You are learning control. But you cannot let rage dictate your decisions again."

Pan exhaled shakily, resting his forehead briefly against Bell's folded wings. The surge of power he had felt atop Hook's ship—rage, vindication, justice—was intoxicating, but now it was replaced by exhaustion and the crushing weight of what he had done. His gaze fell to the floor, to the wet canvas of the tent, and he felt the enormity of his own impulsiveness for the first time.

Bell stirred, a soft flutter of wings, a faint murmur escaping her lips. Pan's head shot up. Relief surged, almost painful in its intensity. He pressed a hand over hers. "I'm here," he whispered, voice raw. "I'm not leaving you. You're safe. I promise."

The elder healer nodded toward Tiger Lily. "She'll rest. Keep her calm. Her magic is fragile still, but stable. She'll awaken fully soon."

Pan nodded, looking at the young archers and Lost Boys waiting outside the tent, then back to Tiger Lily. "We need to move," he said. "Hook's men aren't gone. There's still the lagoon to secure, the remainder of the island…"

Tiger Lily gave him a long, measured look. "And you will lead them," she said quietly, "without letting anger consume you. You have the fire, Peter, but now you need the control."

Pan's jaw tightened, resolve settling in his chest. He looked down at Bell, then over to the boys and the clan. His impulsiveness, his recklessness, had brought them here, but so had his cunning, his leadership, and his determination to protect those he loved. The cost was heavy, but the path forward was clear.

He rose to his feet, breathing deeply, letting the rain outside mix with the sweat and tears on his face. "All right," he said, voice firm. "We regroup. We protect what remains. And we make sure Neverland never suffers under him—or anyone—again."

Tiger Lily stepped close, her hand brushing his arm in a gesture both grounding and approving. "Then let's begin," she said.

And for the first time that night, Pan felt the full weight of leadership settle into his shoulders—not just the fire of anger, not just the drive to protect, but the clarity of purpose, the hard-won balance between heart and mind, fury and strategy, rage and responsibility.

The storm outside continued, the island itself seeming to hold its breath, waiting to see whether the Prince of Neverland, tempered by love and loss, would rise fully into the role he had been born to claim.

The rain had eased into a fine drizzle by dawn, leaving the forest slick and shining, every leaf trembling with residual moisture. Pan led the Lost Boys and members of Le Clan de L'Aura Radieuse through the underbrush, moving cautiously toward the dark expanse of Mermaid Lagoon. Their footsteps were quiet, purposeful—Pan's earlier recklessness tempered by hours of reflection, but still alive in the sharpness of his commands.

The lagoon sprawled ahead, mist curling above its surface like ghostly fingers. Hook's men were scattered along the banks, regrouping after their leader's death, uncertain, disoriented. The air smelled of brine, wet moss, and the lingering iron tang of blood.

Pan raised his hand, signaling for the group to halt. Tiger Lily stepped beside him, eyes scanning the treeline. "They're trying to form ranks," she murmured, voice low. "If we push now, they'll collapse."

Pan's gaze hardened. "We do this smart," he said, teeth gritted. "You flank the left. The Lost Boys and archers cover the right. No one goes alone. Keep the children safe in the mountains." His voice carried both authority and the weight of his earlier lessons—the balance of strategy and emotion he'd only begun to grasp.

Arrows sang through the mist, forcing Hook's remaining men to stagger, retreating to the edges of the lagoon. Pan moved like a shadow along the shoreline, eyes sharp, sword at the ready, while Tiger Lily and her guards struck swiftly, dismantling the enemy's formation with precise, merciless efficiency.

It was a brutal ballet of steel and strategy. The Lost Boys moved with coordinated ferocity, inspired by Pan's earlier clarity and tempered impulse. Despite the chaos, Pan felt the weight of his own restraint pressed against him—he wanted to charge recklessly, to cut a path straight to the last of Hook's men, but the memory of Bell's fragile wings and her whispered trust grounded him.

And then—a faint, fluttering sound caught his attention. Bell.

The healers had kept her with them in a secure location at the edge of the forest. The soft glow of her wings shimmered as she slowly stirred, small sparks of her magic flickering to life again. Her eyes opened, hazel pools wary but fierce, and Pan's chest tightened. Relief and longing collided in a burst of adrenaline. He moved quickly to her side, kneeling.

"You're awake," he breathed, voice trembling, hand brushing hers. "You're safe now. I—"

Bell shook her head slightly, a faint smile ghosting her lips despite her weakness. "You... you did it, Peter," she whispered, voice barely audible above the distant shouts of battle. "You stopped him."

Pan's throat tightened. "For you. For everyone. I... I won't let him hurt you again." His hand lingered on hers, grounding him even as the chaos of the skirmish swirled nearby.

The archers from the mountains sent a hail of arrows to cover the retreating pirates, buying Pan's forces time to press forward without exposing the children. The younger boys hid low among the rocks, faces pale but eyes wide with trust in Pan's leadership.

Pan turned back to Tiger Lily. "We need to secure the lagoon fully," he said, voice firm, determination sharpening with every heartbeat. "Once the archers are in position, we press. Everyone moves together—no one splits."

Tiger Lily nodded, respecting the combination of calculated strategy and the emotional gravity driving Pan. "You've grown," she said quietly. "You're learning what it truly means to lead."

As Pan's forces advanced, he glanced back at Bell one last time, her fragile wings pulsing faintly with returning magic. The sight grounded him, a tether to the world outside rage and vengeance. No matter the outcome of this battle, he had a reason to fight beyond himself: for her, for the Lost Boys, for the fragile, magical world of Neverland.

And for the first time, Pan realized that the lessons Hook had twisted and manipulated for years—the balance of strategy, discipline, and instinct—could now be wielded on his own terms, tempered by love, loyalty, and the weight of real responsibility.

The storm had passed, but the battle was only beginning. Pan lifted his sword high, voice echoing across the mist: "For Neverland! For Bell! Forward!"

The Lost Boys and the clan surged with him, an unstoppable tide of fire, steel, and magic, pressing into the lagoon with the precision and ferocity of a storm unleashed.

Chapter 46: Homecoming

The forest around Hangman's Tree felt impossibly quiet after the chaos at Mermaid Lagoon. Mist still curled low among the roots, leaves slick with rain, the distant cries of retreating pirates fading into memory. Pan led the way, sword sheathed but ready, every step measured, eyes scanning for danger. Behind him, the Lost Boys and the clan followed in tight formation, injured and exhausted but alive.

When they arrived at the clearing where Bell had been resting, Pan's chest tightened. She lay on a soft bed of moss and woven blankets, her glittering wings faintly pulsing with the last remnants of magic. An elder of the clan knelt nearby, murmuring incantations, hands glowing with soft green and gold light as they replenished her strength.

Pan dropped to his knees beside her, careful not to disturb the fragile pulse of her wings. "Bell," he whispered, voice catching. She stirred, eyelids fluttering open to reveal hazel eyes bright with cautious relief.

"You made it," she murmured, voice still thin but steady. Her gaze searched his, and in that instant, all the exhaustion, all the chaos, all the fear of loss, melted into something taut and unspoken between them.

Pan's hands brushed hers, trembling slightly. "I promised. I promised I'd protect you... protect all of us. I—" He swallowed, choking on emotion. "I won't let them take you, not ever."

Bell's lips curved in a faint smile, and she squeezed his hand weakly. "You've changed, Peter. You've learned control... but not the part that makes you less... you. You've kept the fire."

He exhaled slowly, letting the tension leave his shoulders, though the weight of the battle and the lives lost still pressed against him. The Lost Boys began regrouping around the clearing, cautious but relieved, whispering among themselves, watching the gentle glow of Bell's wings return.

Tiger Lily stepped forward, her eyes meeting Pan's with quiet authority. "You led them well," she said, voice soft but firm. "The balance of strategy and instinct... you've learned it."

Pan nodded, glancing once more at Bell. "I couldn't have done it without her," he said quietly. "Without a reason to fight."

The elder stayed with Bell as Pan had requested, their magic stabilizing the fairy, ensuring her recovery continued. The archers had guided the younger boys safely back from the mountains, keeping them hidden from any remnants of Hook's forces, while the clan tended to the wounded and reinforced the camp's defenses.

For the first time since the battle had begun, Pan allowed himself to feel the weight of his choices—not just the victories, but the risks he had taken, the moments he had nearly lost control. His impulsiveness had nearly cost Bell, nearly cost the boys—but tempered now by clarity, purpose, and the tether of love, he had survived, and so had the people who mattered most.

He crouched beside Bell, brushing a strand of wet hair from her face. "I'll never let anything like this happen again," he whispered, voice low, almost a vow. Her fingers laced with his, weak but certain, grounding him in a world beyond rage and strategy.

And in that quiet, magical clearing, amidst the hum of restored life and the soft glow of fairy wings, Pan felt the fragile balance he had fought so hard to achieve—between fire and restraint, vengeance and protection, the reckless boy he had been and the leader he had become.

He looked to the horizon where the mist of Mermaid Lagoon still lingered, imagining the battles yet to come, and knew with absolute certainty that whatever awaited them next, they would face it together, tethered not by fear or obligation, but by trust, love, and the hard-earned lessons of Neverland.

Chapter 47: The Hollow Tree

The first golden light of morning filtered through the canopy of Neverland's forest, glinting off dew-soaked leaves and casting long, dappled shadows across the clearing. Pan stood atop a low hill, eyes sweeping the camp below.

The Lost Boys moved among the tents and fires with laughter and ease, their energy unbound yet disciplined, a reflection of the balance he had worked so hard to cultivate. Even in the chaos of their everyday antics — climbing, racing, swinging through the trees — there was a rhythm, a sense of order in freedom.

Pan's gaze fell on Bell, her wings shimmering with renewed brilliance as she moved among the children and the clan members, sharing stories and laughter. Her recovery had been miraculous, the healers of Le Clan de L'Aura Radieuse marveling at how quickly the last traces of Hook's corruption had been purged from her.

She caught Pan's eye from across the clearing, and the faint smile she gave him was full of quiet triumph — a reflection of both the battles they had survived and the life they were building anew.

The air smelled of wildflowers and wet earth, the lingering scent of rain mingling with the sweet tang of healing herbs. Neverland itself seemed to breathe easier, lighter, freed from Hook's shadow. Streams ran clearer, the mined cliffs and waterways slowly returning to their natural, vibrant state.

The creatures that had fled during the conflict began to emerge again, drawn by the balance being restored. Birds filled the sky in brilliant flocks, while pixies danced in the sunbeams, their laughter chiming like bells through the trees.

Pan descended the hill, boots crunching over moss and damp leaves, and greeted the Lost Boys with a broad grin. "Alright, you lot, breakfast first, then we've got practice!" His voice carried a lightness, the carefree authority of a leader who knew both the value of discipline and the power of joy.

A few of the older boys, those who had fought bravely at Mermaid Lagoon, fell into step beside him. "You handled that ambush like a pro, Pan," one said, eyes alight. "You were... unstoppable."

Pan chuckled, shaking his head. "Unstoppable? Nah. I nearly got myself killed a few times, thanks to a certain mentor of mine," he said with a teasing glance toward the treeline where the forest seemed to hold whispers of Hook's lessons. "But we've learned, haven't we? Balance, patience... and maybe a little restraint."

Tiger Lily emerged from the tent, walking with the poised authority that had earned Pan's utmost respect. "You've grown," she said quietly, meeting his gaze. "You've taken the fire that once ruled you and shaped it into something stronger. The boys trust you, and so do the clan."

Pan nodded, his thoughts flickering briefly to the lessons Hook had taught him — strategy, precision, and the dangerous allure of control. But now those lessons were tempered by his instincts, his love for Neverland, and his care for the people who relied on him. He could wield them without being consumed by them, wield them to protect, not dominate.

Below, the younger boys scampered through the trees, Bell's laughter ringing out as she raced to match them. She paused, skimming the treetops with her wings, before landing gracefully beside Pan. "The lagoon looks healthier today," she said, brushing a hand against his arm. "The mines are sealed, the creatures are returning... and the children are safe."

Pan smiled, feeling a lightness he hadn't known since Hook's shadow first fell over the island. "It's all coming back," he said, voice low, almost reverent. "The magic... the balance... Neverland is healing."

A messenger from the clan approached, a small bundle of letters clutched in her hands. "News from the villagers and those freed from Hook's grasp," she said. "They're starting to rebuild… families reunited, trade returning, and the magic is flowing again."

Pan's chest swelled with pride and relief. The boy who had once raced recklessly through the forest, guided only by instinct and impulse, now stood as the protector of a world slowly knitting itself back together. He glanced at the Lost Boys, at Tiger Lily, at Bell — and for the first time, he felt the weight of responsibility not as a burden, but as a mantle he was proud to wear.

He knelt briefly to tie a young boy's boot, then vaulted up into the trees, landing beside Bell who had taken the lead for a playful race among the branches. "Try to keep up!" she teased.

Pan laughed, chasing her through the canopy, swinging with abandon, but this time every movement was grounded in purpose. He was free to be the boy of Neverland, the fearless leader, the protector — and no shadow, no mentor from the past, could take that from him.

And as the sun rose higher, illuminating the forest in gold, Pan knew that Neverland's story was far from over. But for now, it was safe, alive, and vibrant, and its protector, its leader, its heart, had finally found his own balance.

Chapter 48: The Heart of Neverland

The stars shimmered above Neverland like scattered jewels, their light drifting across the calm waters of Mermaid Lagoon. The moon hung low and soft, brushing the trees with silver, and the island pulsed with quiet life — the hum of crickets, the distant murmur of waves, the gentle whisper of wind through the leaves.

Pan sat at the edge of the lagoon, one knee drawn up, a small smile tugging at his lips as he watched the reflection of the night sky ripple over the surface. Beside him, Bell rested against his shoulder, her wings faintly aglow — not the weak, fading light of a dying fairy, but the warm, steady radiance of one reborn.

"Never thought we'd get nights like this again," Pan said softly, tossing a pebble into the water. "Quiet ones."

Bell chuckled, her voice like the shimmer of starlight itself. "You always say you don't like quiet."

"I don't," Pan admitted, grinning. "But this kind... I can live with."

Behind them, the Lost Boys had gathered around a small fire, roasting fish and roots, laughter echoing

through the clearing. The clan was there too —
warriors and healers mingling freely with the boys,
music drifting on the breeze from a handmade flute.
Tiger Lily stood at the edge of the camp, arms
folded, watching them with the faintest of smiles.

It had been months since the fall of Hook's ship.
Months since the mines had been filled in, the
waters purified, the forests allowed to regrow. The
balance of magic, once bleeding out of the island
like lifeblood, had begun to heal. Neverland was
alive again — not as it had been before, but
something newer, wiser, stronger.

The freed captives of Hook's camp had made their
homes with the clan, their laughter once more
echoing across the glades. The creatures that had
hidden in the deep woods and shadowed caves
now roamed freely, their eyes gleaming with trust
instead of fear. Even the air itself felt cleaner,
charged with energy that hummed beneath the
skin.

Pan leaned back on his hands, gazing up at the
constellations he'd named as a boy — some for
fallen friends, others for dreams he'd long since
outgrown. "They say the stars remember
everything," he murmured. "Even the bad parts."

"They do," Bell said. "But they shine brighter for the
good ones."

For a long while, they simply watched the lagoon, listening to the quiet joy around them. Pan felt it all — the peace, the laughter, the weight of the island's heartbeat thrumming in time with his own. He had learned to carry it not as a burden, but as belonging.

The glow of the lagoon shimmered softly across Bell's face, the light of a thousand fireflies reflected in her eyes. She turned toward him, her expression gentle, almost unreadable. For a moment, neither spoke. The world seemed to shrink to the quiet space between them — the soft lap of water against the shore, the hush of the wind moving through the reeds.

"You've changed," Bell murmured, her voice light but edged with warmth. "You're not the same boy who used to laugh at danger just to see if it would flinch."

Pan's lips curved faintly, though his eyes stayed on her. "Maybe I just learned what's worth protecting."

Bell's hand brushed against his, their fingers tangling, a simple touch that carried all the words they hadn't said. The air between them felt alive again — that familiar hum of magic, of connection. Slowly, Bell rose on her toes, her wings catching the faintest shimmer of moonlight, and pressed her lips to his.

The kiss was soft — the kind that didn't rush, didn't demand, but simply existed, like the island itself breathing through them. Her warmth met his steadiness, her light meeting the weight of everything he carried. For the first time in what felt like forever, Pan let himself lean into it, into her, into the fragile, fierce comfort of being seen.

When they finally parted, their foreheads rested together, breaths mingling. Bell smiled faintly, her voice barely a whisper. "You don't have to carry everything alone anymore, Pan."

He exhaled, a quiet laugh escaping. "I don't think I could, even if I tried. You'd never let me."

Before Bell could respond, the sound of laughter drifted across the lagoon — the boys, starting up a song by the fire. Rough voices, mismatched but joyful, echoed through the trees. Bell chuckled softly, pulling back just enough to meet his eyes.

"Duty calls," she teased.

Pan stood, brushing the dirt from his trousers, his grin returning — freer, lighter, something closer to the boy he once was. "Aye. But I'll come back."

"You'd better," Bell said, her tone playful but her gaze lingering on him, soft as moonlight.

Pan gave a small nod before stepping away toward the song, the laughter of the boys wrapping around the night. And for the first time in a long while, everything — the island, the magic, the people he loved — felt whole again.

"Tomorrow," he called to the camp, his grin wide, "we fly to the cliffs at dawn! There's a sunrise there even Bell says rivals her wings!"

The boys cheered, Bell swatted him playfully, and Tiger Lily shook her head, laughing under her breath.

As the laughter died down, Bell turned to him, eyes glowing softly. "You've changed, Pan."

"Maybe," he said, glancing toward the horizon where the first hints of dawn began to stir. "But not too much. Someone's got to keep the island on its toes."

She smiled, leaning in close. "Then may you always stay just wild enough."

Pan smirked, wings of light catching in Bell's reflection. "And you — don't ever stop keeping me in check."

They stood together as the first rays of morning painted the sky in gold and rose. The world of Neverland stretched before them — alive, breathing, whole. The battles were done, the shadows gone. What remained was laughter, light, and the eternal heartbeat of the island that would never grow old.

And at its center stood Pan — still wild, still free, still the boy who led the lost.
 But now, finally, also the man who had found his purpose.